Twilight Troubadour

Also by Robert Franklin Gish

Bad Boys and Black Sheep:Fateful Tales From the West
Beautiful Swift Fox: Erna Fergusson and the Modern Southwest
Beyond Bounds: Cross-Cultural Essays on Anglo,
      American Indian, and Chicano Literature
Dreams of Quivira: Stories in Search of the Golden West
First Horses: Stories of the New West
Frontier's End: The Life and Literature of Harvey Fergusson
Hamlin Garland: The Far West
Nueva Granada: Paul Horgan and the Southwest
Paul Horgan
Retold Native American Myths
River of Ghosts: A Cedar Valley Odyssey
Songs of My Hunter Heart: A Western Kinship
West Bound: Stories of Providence
When Coyote Howls: A Lavaland Fable
William Carlos Williams: A Study of The Short Fiction

Twilight Troubadour

Stories Serenading the American Southwest

Robert Franklin Gish

SUNSTONE
PRESS

SANTA FE

The characters portrayed in these stories are projections of the author's imagination.

Sunstone books may be purchased for educational, business, or sales promotional use. For information please write: Special Markets Department, Sunstone Press, P.O. Box 2321, Santa Fe, New Mexico 87504-2321.

Book and cover design › R. Ahl
Printed on acid-free paper
∞

———————————

Library of Congress Cataloging-in-Publication Data

Names: Gish, Robert, author.
Title: Twilight troubadour : stories serenading the American Southwest / by Robert Franklin Gish.
Description: Santa Fe : Sunstone Press, [2019]
Identifiers: LCCN 2019006383 | ISBN 9781632932594 (pbk. : alk. paper)
Classification: LCC PS3557.I79 A6 2019 | DDC 813/.54--dc23
LC record available at https://lccn.loc.gov/2019006383

———————————

WWW.SUNSTONEPRESS.COM
SUNSTONE PRESS / POST OFFICE BOX 2321 / SANTA FE, NM 87504-2321 /USA
(505) 988-4418 / ORDERS ONLY (800) 243-5644 / FAX (505) 988-1025

To Matt, Joe, Daniel, Mia, Aoife, Cash, and Enzo

Contents

Acknowledgments

The assistance of many persons is needed in writing stories such as these. I wish to thank the following individuals for their information, comments, assistance, and encouragement: Clemencia Cisneros-Olivas, Rachel Lukes, Daniel Portell; Bill and Mike Glassnapp, Bruce Grove, Rodolfo Gonzales, Darlene Vigil, and James Clois Smith, Jr.

Most of all, I am grateful for the support of Judith, my wife; Robin, Tim, and Annabeth, our children; and our seven grandchildren—all loves of my life.

Gratitude also needs expressing to Bix, our ever loyal, always searching English setter.

Preface

My wife likes to hurry me along with the phrase, "Let's go so we can get back." It's a fine admonition for a dawdler. What's missed in between the going and the getting back is often surpassed by the excitement of departure and return. Paradoxically, life's hellos and goodbyes seem to expand and accelerate with the passing of time and even in attempts to lose oneself in arrival, the present, the "now" of the ancient though repackaged popularity of mindfulness. Memories and age are a kind of twilight, much worthy of a troubadour.

The Roman deity of doorways, Janus, had the pleasure and, presumably, the pain, of seeing both past and future, a special kind of prolonged yet exasperating present allowing what some have called "memories of the future." The trouble is that among other pitfalls in such a paradox, memories are fallible and reality is in some sense mostly illusion, making autobiography a malleable vessel.

This, however, is where fiction and memoir cross, and the ethnocentric thought that most imaginative literature could be seen as a footnote to Plato, that the novel and, one might add, quest stories are ultimately indebted to chivalric romance, to Cervantes, and to his either misinformed or enlightened dreamer, Don Quixote, and to his pragmatically brilliant companion Sancho Panza.

Herman Hesse's observations that "History is as it has happened," and that "History's third dimension is always fiction" tease one into both the frustration and consolation that our lives as we remember or tell them or post them on Facebook are not necessarily the lives we live, certainly not the lives others think we live.

The telling and showing of history, biography, autobiography, memoir, and their narrative cousin, fiction, confuse "fact" so profoundly as to leave one believing, whether in the coming or the going, that life is indeed a dream, that all the world's a stage, that we merely act the roles we are given or that we assign. The loss of memory is a terrible curse known to all too many families these days as they watch loved ones grope to recognize even the closest, most familiar of faces.

Perhaps William Carlos Williams's assertion that "Memory is a kind/Of accomplishment/A sort of Renewal," is our best hope for opening "new places." Such is the blessing of remembering and thereby renewing a life, or lives, through our retelling, our reshaping what might have happened but never really did until the telling. Telling "lies," intended or unintended, after all, is as important, biographers keenly know, as telling "lives." And our lies, everyone knows, our befuddlements and "muddledoms" (as E.M. Forster calls them) afford us an out, a blessing, a renewal. This, perhaps, is the "supreme fiction"—what William Blake calls the "sweet mercy" blessing of living and of remembering, of our ascent and descent, of going and of getting back, of blessing and being blessed. Not only mercy, as Shakespeare suggests, but memory "blesseth him that gives, and him that takes." We are thus "twice blest," both in the living and in the telling.

"History's third dimension is always fiction."
—Hermann Hesse, *The Glass Bead Game*

Twilight Troubadour

"Heavenly shades of night are falling. It's twilight time."
—Buck Ram, Morty Nevins, Al Nevins, Artie Dunn, "Twilight Time"

Jerry would talk about lots of things during our lessons. Sure, he'd talk about the guitar, chords and notes and tempo and such, but he'd also talk about his life, his loves, especially Margaret, his adventures, his highs and his lows as the music of his days would play out. It all related to melody somehow, at least that's what I figured out after a while, a kind of soul serenade you might say.

The guitar was the way in and out of such revelations, for the instrument itself would open up some of its secrets now and then and pretty much play itself through you. A guitar was just like a pen or a typewriter...it played what you told it to play. Jerry said we played ourselves through the guitar, but I'm pretty sure it worked both ways. Some days you were in tune, just like the guitar, and some days you were out of tune. One day the guitar was new and kept all its music to itself, then one day the guitar was scratched and dinged, giving, but cracked and in need of repair. Just like Jerry—and just like me. I learned the hard way about the need for sweet mercy for a guitar and loving mercy for friends.

It wasn't long after I got it—brand shiny new with its beautiful brown-yellow, sunburst finish and its gold Gibson lettering on the headstock, and its pearl dot inlays on the neck and its eager bright sounding strings, not long at all, before I cracked it. In frustration, after I couldn't make it sound right, I slammed it on the floor, right on the end pin and cracked it. It was used, "Damaged goods," as they say. Yet it was really new.

It was new and it was cracked and I was young and frustrated, a bit like Jerry in his wilder days, I guess. His guitar had been pretty much played through, worn down with friction and with sweat stains. It only revived its luster when Jerry played it. And boy that guy could play the guitar! He played an arch-top Spanish guitar with dulled finish and fingernail tracks all over the pick guard and big flakes of varnish chipped off the back where his belt buckle scratched the finish every time he held it close to him. It was a Gibson too, an expensive, blonde Super 400 to be exact, though I couldn't tell a Harmony from a Washburn, a Martin from an Epiphone back then. I had only some vague notion about quality craftsmanship.

He told me all about it, of course. By quality I mean not only naming and describing the parts of his guitar (and mine too) as we went along: the tuning keys, the bridge, the tail piece, the neck and frets, the headstock and the Sitka spruce top and fine curly-maple back—even the serial number and markings you could see through the "f" holes if you looked real close. He even told me how he had special ordered his guitar and had his initials inlayed in mother of pearl on the frets: JJ for Jerry Jenkins. It was a beautiful looking and sounding guitar, made all the more beautiful by the wear, tear, and careless care.

It meant the world to Jerry and you could tell that the minute he took it out of the case where he kept it covered with a white silk handkerchief with a colorful Chinese design on it—several farmers irrigating and cultivating a rice paddy. I don't know what the lettering meant, something about how you need to grow the rice slowly and cook it even slower in the dark, according to Jerry. He said the handkerchief was given to him by Margaret—his girl friend who used to dance with it and used it as a kind of veil. She was an exotic dancer and he said she danced lovingly just like a geisha, whatever that meant. But she wasn't Japanese or anyone Asian, as I soon learned.

"She's what some like to call a "stripper," he said—performing out in the canyon east of town at the Paradise Club and on the west mesa's Central Avenue at the Club Chesterfield. Her favorite song, he said, was "Twilight Time," and that she knew every special move—hands, body, you name it—for every melody, pickup, and turn-around line to that song. He taught it to me later on as soon as I could handle it, what with all the tough chord changes. He said, "Rory, if you just relax and go to the basement of your soul it's easier to play than eating with chopsticks."

I didn't quite understand what he meant but I tried to do it—go deep into myself, way down past the basement of my mind into my soul, I guess it was.

He'd have me sing along and he'd punctuate the key phrases with "boom, boom" to illustrate how Margaret would bump and grind out her moves. Then he'd improvise a chorus with a flourish of his hands, just like he was dancing with his love—his guitar become Margaret, Margaret become guitar. Her professional name was once "Gina Sing," he said, but now she was known as "Catalina," and laughed at all the one-dollar bills she carried, so many and so typically that he sometimes laughingly referred to her as "Gorgeous George."

I didn't know what he meant by that at first but then he explained that most of her tips of admiration were dollar bills, and she'd have to count them up and then change them out at the bank or hold up the customer lines at stores while she counted them out at the register. "I call my guitar "Gorgeous George" too, more in her honor of Margaret than President Washington" and his ax.

Then he explained how George Washington chopped down a cherry tree with an ax and that a guitar was called an ax too because of chops and licks lingo. So George was a fitting name since the wood that made the guitar had been chopped down too at one time. Early on Jerry let me play old George and I could really tell how great and true he really was since even with frightened, unsure fingers the strings jumped right up to meet me.

§

How I came to know Jerry and have him for a teacher isn't so much the story, although I'm sure he'd have his own take on trying to teach a kid the finer points of six-string musicianship, as it is my story—or I guess more accurately our story.

Anyway, I'd always liked music, and particularly Western music, since my father knew Bob Wills back in Oklahoma, or said he did, claiming that my uncle had married Bob Wills' sister or cousin or someone. So I always heard my dad singing Bob Wills songs, especially "Oozlin' Daddy Blues," and "Take Me Back to Tulsa," plus, Dad aspired to be a first-class square-dance caller and was always listening to Cliffy Stone recordings and singing out "dosado" and "promenades" to "Ida Red," calls like "Chicken in the bread pan pickin' out dough," "Granny does your dog bite, no child no," and such poetry. I even took piano lessons for a time from an old recluse lady out on Barcelona Road and learned to read notes and name the black and white keys and marveled at how my sister knocked off a Franz Liszt or a Chopin tune with ease on the family upright. And how my Okie aunt whimsically accompanied by ear a bunch of homegrown cloggers.

But Merle Travis and the three Hanks: Williams, Snow, and Thompson, were my kind of guys, and all three (maybe not so much Hank Williams) could play the heck out of a guitar, be it flat top or Spanish electric. So I kept begging for a guitar and the way I got one and then got Jerry as a teacher were pure luck, I guess.

I'd better tell you one more thing about music and me, but I'm not proud to tell it. In my mother's café there was this beautiful jukebox and along the edges of the counters were coin boxes with little flip menus and you could drop a nickel in the slot and magically the jukebox would select and turn and drop and spin a 78 record of choice. But this one time it got stuck and wouldn't drop on Hank Snow's "I've Been Everywhere Boy," so I go over to the jukebox, all carnival red, glowing yellow and Shamrock green but kind of blinking and sputtering, so I tap—okay, hit, the glass to try and dislodge whatever is lodged. It wasn't a hard tap, at least not the first one. But on the third hit the glass breaks and the lights short out and I have what must have been a stroke or a heart attack or something because next thing I know I'm on the hard, highly polished, glass strewn tile floor. And people are standing over me, especially Hot Shot and the cook, Mrs. Curly—and my mother. I get a scolding once I'm back on my feet and told to hide out while they call the jukebox repairman.

So I seek solace up on the roof, which wasn't hard to get to, given a big steel-pipe staircase installed out the back door for just that purpose. While I'm up there I start to philosophize about accidents and what just happened and how Hank Snow and his picking techniques were somehow responsible and that I would eventually have to really pay the price, whatever that was, for what I'd just done. So I start to sing a few verses of some sad Hank Williams songs like "Got a Feelin' Called the Blues," "I'm So Lonesome I Could Cry," "Lovesick Blues," and one I was learning and really liked called "Lost Highway." Because that's what I was on, a lost highway and I'd better stop my glass breaking ways or I'd be far gone—just "ramblin' round."

I was feeling pretty sorry for myself but enjoying the solitude of the roof and the consolations of song, when the Juke Box repair guy drives up in his Lincoln, complete with a continental kit on the back. He was a black guy. He looked a lot like Prince Bobby Jack whom Jerry told me about and who performed out on the West side at the Peacock Lounge. "Nobody gives Bobby any guff!" Jerry said. "Nobody!" Hearing those stories I was sure I'd be a straight razor fricassee before nightfall. Anyway, this repair guy stays for an eternity, enough time for me to be sliced, diced, and ground up into meatballs, and I stop my singing, even under my breath, fearful of being found out. But he leaves and I'm called back to human society, and climb down to take a very heavy but oh so welcome scolding.

Funny thing is this: when my dad heard about it, he just said, "Son, I'm buying you that goddamn guitar you keep asking about so you don't have to depend on breaking your mom's jukebox for entertainment."

§

"Hot damn for Bobby Jack and Hank Snow!" was all I could say, and the very next day I found myself in May's Music Store on Central talking not only to Bernie May himself but this short little guy they introduce me to named Mel Tormé.

"Mel here is quite the popular pianist and vocalist. They call him the Velvet Fog, pipes up Bernie—all suited up to the minute complete with narrow "V" knot tie and a starched white shirt with treble clef cuff links. "Been in movies and is a recording star out in Hollywood. Lead vocalist for the Mel-Tones," Bernie keeps jabbering. "We have his latest seventy-eight."

Then Bernie turns to my mother and says, "Maybe Rory here will turn out like Mel if he practices his piano and takes some voice lessons." I didn't register much, but then Mel Tormé, the Velvet Fog himself, who was just about my height, a little guy for a grown man, like I said, reaches over and with a Foggy-Froggy smile and his talented fingers tousles my hair.

"Hear that kid. All it takes is practice—and a big dose of talent!"

The more he talked I did begin to hear and see why they called him the Velvet Fog. He had a smooth but kind of croaky voice and he looked kind of like a frog—his lips and ears and even his hands. "The Velvet Frog," I started to think to myself. I could imagine him leaping into a pond saying "ribbet, ribbet." I didn't know what a "big dose of talent was" but Jerry confided in me that he once had a "big dose of the clap" but was over it now, and I should watch out for that. I thought at first he meant something about clapping and applause—but I was wrong there. And talent? Well, I don't know about Mel, but that was what Hank had, and Jerry too—"talent." The kind of thing my bible school friends said, advising that we shouldn't keep our talents under a bushel basket. They misunderstood the Bible.

So we get a nice enveloped "Decca Jazz" recording of Mel's latest song about falling dead leaves, "Autumn Leaves" was the title if you can believe it, and then we're turned over to a guy named Hal Stone, I thought I heard his name pronounced "Hail Storm," although I was wrong there. His real name was Harold Strong. He was the guitar salesman specially assigned to us for the historic transaction of "buying this boy a guitar." The big question was, "Which one would lead me to becoming the next Merle Travis or Mel Tormé, and at what price?"

Well, we see a whole bunch of different guitars in different sizes and colors, some with wire-wound strings, some with nylon strings, some acoustic and some electric. I fell for a Gibson flattop. It had a round sound hole, pearl dot inlays, a tortoise shell pick guard and was a nice size and shape. Inside the sound hole I saw it was made in Kalamazoo, Michigan and it had a pretty low serial number as such things go, which Hal said was a good thing, making for a good investment over the years. The price was low too, right at $100.00, which we could pay out in installments—good news music to my mother.

So we got it, along with a multi-colored braided neck strap so you could play your guitar standing up when serenading. Hal brought up the fact that guys who serenaded girls were popular and never had sand kicked in their face over at Tingley Beach or strolling through the zoo. I could just picture myself singing to the zoo animals, especially the monkeys and thought of my burro, Jack's, attempts at singing on our rides. I could see myself like Tex Ritter or maybe Gene Autry, strumming to the clopping rhythms of my road rides. Then there was also that story about the Bremen Town Musicians all grouped as a barnyard chorus, bringing new meaning to "country music." But imagining Jack sitting down on my new guitar ruined the mood.

As I left the store, carrying my new guitar in its new soft-shell case, Mel salutes me from one of the listening booths and pretends to strum an imaginary guitar, giving me an okay sign. He wasn't such a bad guy and later when we listened to the record he gave us, he sounded kind of soft and feminine but pretty good, being able to hit some really high notes, then some low notes and kind of hum and imitate leaves falling. I decided right then and there, however, to call my guitar "Hank" not "Mel" in honor of my guitar pickin' heroes.

Anyway, my father got the notion to call up Dick Bills, this guy with a first name for a last name, and the leader of the Sandia Mountain Boys and ask if he gave guitar and singing lessons. He had his own weekly TV show on "K Circle B" he called it, instead of KOB, and my dad had heard him talk once at the Lions Club. "Branding Iron Bills," dad called him.

"Glad to help an Okie, real glad to help, Hoss. Okies and Texans got to stick together. My lead guitarist is the man, Jerry Jenkins. Had some trouble with the bottle and replaced him for a time with my nephew who's now in California. I'll have Jerry call you."

He did and Jerry came out to the house one day and introduced himself to my dad who ushered him back to the living quarters behind the cafe for a first lesson. He had his guitar with him, still in its beat up case, but with the initials "JJ" painted on the top. I had my guitar out and was ready.

Jerry was a tall guy and had long strawberry-blonde hair, not like a girl or anything but long over his ears and on his neck. He never let a barber shave around his ears or the back of his neck—that was obvious. He had some freckles but not too many and kind of faded, like he'd tried to bleach them out or something since, I could tell, some freckles were darker and better outlined than others. He reminded me more of a thin Arthur Godfrey, who, by the way, played a silly ukulele and not a guitar, which, I guess, was all right. Jerry was about twice as tall as the Velvet Fog, and was dressed all in black. He wore a western style shirt, black but with a soft caramel-colored yoke, with gold ribbing. He wore a bolo tie with an inlayed turquoise Kokopelli. His boots were kind of scuffed up but had tiny engraved silver tips on the toes.

We hit if off right away because he said, "How about a song first thing?" and he took that big blonde archtop guitar of his out of its case, laid his big freckled palms and long-fingered hands on it and began to sing a tune called "Blue Eyes Cryin' in the Rain," all about broken hearts and rain and tears which I recognized right away, having seen lots of people cry, including myself. Then he played a chord melody straight out of heaven. I could tell while I watched his hands that he chewed his fingernails. You know, you could see the quick beneath them. He used a pick for the most part, but now and then put it between his lips and played softly with his thumb and fingers. There was a mixture of smoke and whiskey on his breath and in his music.

When he finished, he said, "You want to try, Rory? Just three chords and they ain't hard." So he helped me put my fingers on the right strings, just the top three strings that time, and pretty soon, through the hurt in the tips of my virgin fingers, I was strumming along—nothing fancy, you understand, but I was strumming and Jerry was singing. And then he nodded his head for me to join in on the words. Well, it was quite the feeling and soon I could almost keep up with him, although he'd slowed everything down to a crawl. You could smell the whiskey strong on his breath, like the Old Crow smell on my father's breath from time to time, especially around Christmas when he liked it with eggnog. And to tell you the truth whiskey smells really good. I thought to myself, "I'll call him the Velvet Crow instead of the Velvet Frog." I didn't tell him that, of course. Just a nickname I gave him, private like.

He left me an old tattered music book, entitled "Foggy River and Other Songs" with the chords and words to several songs, and told me to work on them since the chords were diagrammed at the top of each line and said, "See you next time, little guy." I peeked through the Venetian blinds to see him get in his car, an old Packard—which had Sandia Mountain Boys painted on the door over an outline of some mountains—and I saw him peel out and swerve from the side of the house back on to the paved street.

After a few lessons I knew the chords to several songs, including "Wabash Cannonball," "Faded Love," and "Foggy River." I wondered how Mel, the Velvet Fog, would sing it. But I knew how Jerry sang it and more about him too. He'd come in the café and try his luck punching out all the holes in the punchboard, then he'd order a cheeseburger and a suicide coke (every syrup in the fountain) or maybe a bowl of chile with crackers and I'd pretty much order the same—maybe a hamburger with all the trimmings and a chocolate malt with a raw egg in it and we'd sit at the café counter or in a booth, play some jukebox tunes, and talk. Just for the fun of it he taught me how to make a pickle sandwich by placing a pickle slice between two potato chips. I guess those scrumptious and fun meals were a kind of bonus payment for his $5.00 lesson fee. He taught me how to blow the wrapper off a straw and sail it like an airplane. Jerry was loaded with talent. Oh, and pecan pie. He loved pecan pie with a cup of Farmer Brothers coffee.

§

One day Margaret came around with him and I picked up some life-changing information. I guess she felt a bit embarrassed around mother and the waitresses. Mrs. Curly seemed generally grumpy and disapproving of the company I was keeping. But it was all worth it to me.

"Rory," Margaret asks me, is that your real name or did you change it to impress your friends, a way of saying you were someone special?"

After saying that it was my real name she started telling me about how she first came to be "Gina Sing" (said she took it off a tea bag), and then "Catalina" there at the club and that Jerry was really Gerald and that lots of movie stars changed their names just for popularity sake and that a name didn't just have to mean a name but could suggest all kinds of things, just like music. In fact, she informed me, "A name is its own kind of music, Rory dear."

"Margaret," she went on, "is the name of queens and royalty and of very proper ladies. You could shorten it of course to Maggie or something but that's a rather ordinary girl of the streets kind of name, notwithstanding its association with majesty and the like. But Catalina, well, what do you associate with that, other than my present professional name as a dancer?"

She was telling me about Catalina Island which she said was some twenty-six miles off the coast of southern California, and humming a tune about how Santa Catalina was waiting for me, for us all, and how you could get there in a glass-bottomed boat—while Jerry sucked on the ice in his nearly dead suicide coke. I was trying to use some table straws as blow guns, shooting the paper wrappers like Jerry taught me out into the middle of the café when this local customer and neon sign man named Smitty comes in and, spotting our booth, strides right over and says, "Well, Miss Catalina, surprised to see you here at the table with your slow-fingered guitar man—and what's this? With young Master Strayhope in person? Say, Jerry, make your bail bond, did you, and out on parole?"

I see Jerry doesn't like the guy and neither does Catalina, and I never did whenever he came in, and between my shenanigans blowing on straws I catch a blush beneath Margaret's rouged cheeks, all the way down her neck and on into her chest and ample, motherly breasts. Jerry and Margaret just both nod and give Smitty a wave of recognition and keep on talking and sipping their drinks.

"That's not 'Twilight Time' I hear, darlin,' but an appropriate tune even for those of us hoping Miss Catalina is waitin' for us, arms...and all open. Saw your midnight show last Saturday and you left us all wanting more, though there wasn't much more to want—if you get my drift."

Finally Jerry turns and spits some ice back into his glass and stares a ray-gun hole through shitty Smitty who starts to melt like a strawberry sundae somebody forgot to serve, and says, "Mind your manners, Pard, and go blow your neon colors into some long, crooked glass tubes. What happens on weekends doesn't happen here. Can't you see the boy is just making Margaret's acquaintance and we're all having a good, wholesome time. So you're excused, PARD!" But Jerry's tone of voice is pretty sarcastic if not downright threatening and about the time Jerry finishes the word "Pard," pronouncing it hard and hammer like, old Smitty is back peddling and puffing toward the counter and reciting his same old slogan as he grabs a stool: "Got a cup of Java for a poor old beggar?" and he's holding out his hand as usual, except this time it's shaking more than usual like he's been hard hit by palsy.

"What a dumb bastard," Jerry says beneath his breath. "Sorry about that, honey!" And there for a minute I couldn't tell whether he's talking to me or Margaret, or maybe both of us. She's still sitting there looking like she's got a bad sunburn and suddenly she reaches over to hold my hand and smile a smile through those beautiful cherry-coke-red lips that darn near makes me choke on my straw's wrapper and I reach over with my other hand to grab for a drink of water forgetting that it's one of Jerry's custom-made Timber Floats and I almost choke on the toothpick by mistake.

But as I recover enough to take a few sips of ice water I look over and see Smitty is frowning now and talking real serious like to my mother, like he's complaining about the coffee for being stale and scalded.

Jerry gets up and kind of crams his hat on and Margaret follows, pulling up the front of her dress and her brassiere straps, and she waves good bye in a hurry saying nothing until they make it to his big car where I can see lots of agitated talking and gesturing through the soon fogged over windshield.

§

That night in the living room right next to my bedroom I was thinking about Margaret, tea bags, and her breasts, Catalina and her beguiling mouth and smile, and I overhear my parents talking about the Paradise Club and how Catalina dances there and whether or not Jerry's the proper teacher for a young boy. And I hear Dad say, "I'll check it out this weekend, but Jerry's the boy's teacher, not Catalina."

"I wonder about that..." I heard mom say.

I never knew just what my father saw when he went to the Paradise Club to watch and investigate Margaret and her dancing. I know she never came back with Jerry for any talks like before. Jerry told me he stuck around at the club to protect Margaret, and that between shows he had talked to my father and that he had come in one night with Boyd Harper and had a drink and watched Catalina's show. "Pure artistry!" they all agreed, Jerry said. I could only imagine how beautiful and artistic Catalina was in her dancing—so curvaceous and graceful and all, moving to each note of "Twilight Time." I had more than one fantasy about her and the soft but tight texture of her skin and the fullness of her mouth and her kissable lips. I saw her up there on the stage with the colorful lights playing off her costume and her hair and her beautiful pendulous breasts—her arms waving to and fro with that Chinese handkerchief as if to embrace the very peaks and valleys of the Sandia Mountains themselves just as the sunset hit them and turned them watermelon pink with those heavenly shades of nighttime falling—and her gathering all God's creation into her bosom.

But she never came back with Jerry and I only had a few more lessons with him after he taught me how to play a really hard piece called "The Third Man," which I somehow thought was me and that if I wasn't the man Jerry was, or my dad, I was becoming one and that some one like Catalina was out there dancing for me.

I remember still all those real and imagined songs and dances, ever and always interpreted by Catalina and Jerry—and over the years I applied it too. Soon I was serenading every girl I could coax into listening to me. I'd lay on my back, propped up against a tree or my car, softly strum my guitar, and sing "In the twilight glow I see them, blue eyes cryin' in the rain," or "I'll hold you in my heart, 'till I can hold you in my arms, like you've never been held before," or "A cowboy can't reveal, just how bad he feels, so I'll keep riding, hiding teardrops in my heart," or "Remember me when the candle lights are gleaming. Remember me at the close of a long, long day"—sad, lovesick songs usually. Sometimes I'd drive out to the west mesa at twilight and look east toward the mountains, thinking of Jerry and Margaret and where they were, and in every girl's eyes, in every girl's sighs I longed for Catalina, knowing in some way she loved me like I loved her.

Uncle Nabob, Milo, and Me

"I love you so much it hurts!"
—Minnie Pearl

I first met Milo Mackey in Mrs. Gonzales's room there at the old Five Points Elementary School in the South Valley, just off Bridge Street and down Heart Line Road, not far from the Rio Grande and the big irrigation ditch. "Five Points" was a misnomer in most ways but not in the ways that really count. Sure, it was a poor area of the county—west of the river—if you measure things by per capita income, education levels, award-winning architecture and other socioeconomic "metrics," as urban planners might phrase it. But when it came to caring, humanistic teachers trying their damnedest to educate and enlighten, well, Mrs. Gonzales was one of those five point individuals. She gave true meaning to "Heart Line Road."

Admittedly, the schools in the Valley were neglected, even though they were part of the public school system, as were the roads and most of the other civic amenities, including city water, sewers, garbage trucks, and the like. Some people who lived there wanted to be annexed by the city and lobbied for incorporation. Others wanted to retain the rural ambiance where you could keep horses and livestock and not be bothered by municipal regulations.

If you look at it one way, living there was like having the benefit of dual residence in the United States and in Mexico because more people spoke Spanish than English. In another way it seemed like you always fell somewhere in-between, on the margins, one foot in a pothole, one in an arroyo. Most of the county roads were dirt, maybe gravel, and maybe oiled down by truckloads of "disposed," recycled motor oil.

There were plenty of poor people, mostly Mexican-American families, with one or two bedroom ramshackle houses, some built of adobe and some framed up with scrap lumber, along side a smattering of gentrified folks who owned an acre or two of irrigated land, usually alfalfa fields, with quite the rambling "hacienda," kind of like a castle, smack in the middle of their land. In some ways life there was feudalistic—fiefdoms complete with dukes and princes and earls, giving new meaning to what was known since early Spanish settlement as the "Duke City."

Don't get me wrong, there were doctors: MDs, osteopaths, chiropractors, veterinarians, curanderas, psychics, palm readers. And there were pharmacists, dentists, barbers, and businesses galore—cafes, bars, variety stores, grocery stores, shoe shops, pool halls, night clubs, gas stations, automobile garages, body and fender shops, upholstery shops, you name it. There were churches too, of course, usually Catholic but now and again Baptist or Seventh Day Adventist, or some type of evangelical assembly. Our family doctor, Doc Heywood, was an Adventist, always advising us that Saturday was really the important day. He sold Watkins products on the side, no prescription needed, just an order form, cash or check.

The South Valley was its own special community and one never really had to head east across either the Barelas Bridge or the West Central bridge and into the city. But it was easy to do, what with busses and cars buzzing along morning noon and night.

Milo Mackey was a poor kid, just how poor, how perverse, I only later came to find out. You know how it is when you just make friends with someone, enjoying their company and all for who knows what reason at the time and never really understanding the draw, the chemistry, even long after that friendship ends. That's the way it was with Milo and me.

Anyway, one day all of us kids were in that rest time set aside by Mrs. Mary Gonzales. We knew her name was Mary because the principal called her that when he came in to play "The Bells of St. Mary's" on the old upright piano.

"Oh, look kids, it's Mr. Lloyd here to play for us!"

"Are you ready for me, Mary? I'm here to play your favorite song. Ready for me to tickle the keys, kids?"

And Mrs. Gonzales would utter words like "wonderful" and

"Gracias! Bueno! Muy bonita! Si, Si! Muy estimado Señor Lloyd," beaming to the clapping and cheers of her budding concertgoers.

Milo was the only one who never cheered or applauded when Mr. Lloyd came in and promised to "tickle" the ivory.

"Nothing funny to tickle! He's not gonna tickle me for sure. Old Lloyd's no darn Tex Ritter," Milo would utter beneath his breath—seated there in the desk behind me in his grungy, blue and white striped, pillow ticking, urine-stained overalls with only one shoulder strap fastened to a lone, loosely-attached brass button. "Some dirty dog needs to put some glue on his saddle!"

Talk about nothing, Milo's sotto voce grumbling was nothing compared to how he would grouse when we came in from recess to put our heads down and were coaxed to listen attentively to recordings of "Swan Lake," or "Polonaise," complete with Mrs. Gonzales' explanations about ballet or Chopin's patriotism.

Some times Mrs. Gonzales would organize a talent show, and kids would do things like recite the "Gettysburg Address" or a poem like Albert Noyes' "The Highwayman," or Robert Service's " The Cremation of Sam McGee" or play the three string violin like Little Joe Aragon or dance the polka like Dickey Lovato and Sally Pacheco—which was rather sad but funny too, what with his cripple leg and built-up Frankenstein shoe, and Sally with her shriveled right hand. They didn't seem to notice their handicaps, however, and pretty soon we didn't either.

They were quite the pair and inspired all of us to shine when we did "La Raspa" for parents at the end of the year in front of the school, underneath the American flag waving in the fresh, resplendent spring breeze, and the sandhill cranes soaring overhead winging their way along, singing their own song, doing their own aerial dancing.

It was at one of the first talent shows of the school year that Milo got up from his desk, hobbled up to the front of the room, walking bow-legged like he needed a bath, a dusting of cornstarch, and fresh underwear, and belted out his version of Tex Ritter's "Blood on the Saddle."

Milo introduced the song by saying that he'd seen Tex Ritter and his horse, White Flash, on stage at the Kimo theater downtown and that his Uncle Bob had bought Ritter's album, including such sagebrush and cactus classics as "Rye Whisky," "Boll Weevil," and "Bad Brahma Bull." Milo said that old Tex even had his name on the headstock of his guitar and that his horse could do any trick asked of him—plus take a bow and whinny when old Tex asked him to sing with him.

Milo's discourse on Tex wasn't as highbrowed as Mrs. Gonzales on Tchaikovsky and Frédéric Chopin, but Milo's talk was most enlightening and you knew well and good that he wanted to be just like Tex some day. Milo's singing voice wasn't that good though, not deep and raspy like Tex's. One problem seemed to be that Milo needed to blow his nose because you could tell his head was all stuffed up. He had problems that way and one day he even came to class with a bad ear infection and super bad ear ache with something that looked like bloody ear wax dripping down the side of his neck.

"There was blood on the saddle, blood on the ground, a great big puddle of blood all around," came the nasal lyrics, made all the more uncomfortable by the way Milo accented the word "b-l-o-o-d," puffing out his cheeks and blowing out the letter "b," all the time trying to control post-nasal drip and a runny nose. Cory Thomas, the kid who always threw up at lunchtime, usually after eating macaroni and cheese, started calling Milo "The Kotex Kid," laughing and saying that was a sure way to get blood on your saddle. Milo took offense and just about broke Cory's finger, bending it back against itself during a dusty wrestling match out by the monkey bars.

I took up for Milo, felt sorry for him, and invited him to go downtown shopping with my mom and me. She wanted to buy me some shirts and things for this little reading she'd scheduled for me to do in front of the Five Points Women's Club over at fat Mrs. L.C. Frazer's house. I blackmailed my way into getting Milo to tag along, telling mom I'd forgotten how to read and really didn't want to stand up in front of all those old ladies with their tea and cakes, talking about which recipe to include in their Five Points holiday recipe book.

She relented and we picked up Milo at his house on Airway in our big Buick, all the while mother saying how shabby Milo's house looked and I thought I caught her actually turning away when he came out to get in the car, though she was polite enough in her greeting, as was Milo. But when we got downtown and parked the car and started to walk down the street to this really nice store operated by Mr. Mandel, who was so very tall, and Mr. Dreyfus, who was so very short, that when I told Milo we were going to shop at Mutt and Jeff's Big and Small Mercantile Company, he took me for being serious, looking all around at the crowds of people and variety of stores—like he'd never been on Central Avenue before. I'd never seen him so shy and big-eyed. And when my mother told him he'd have to go back and wait in the car he pretty much wilted there in front of us. It was a cruel, heartless thing for her to do. I guess motherly love only goes so far on Central Avenue.

"Rory," she gasped, "that boy, that Milo friend of yours is a disgrace! He smells like urine and I'm not taking him into any store that knows us. You'd swear he had no mother to see to him having clean, decent clothes. His overalls are ready for the dump!"

"But, Mother, he doesn't have a mother. She died and he lives with his father and his sister and their Uncle Nabob," I tried to explain, pleading for her okay for Milo to get to shop with us. "Maybe we could buy him some new clothes," I remember saying as I waved to him back in the car. With him singing, "If the Ocean was whisky and I was a duck, I'd dive to the bottom and never come up."

That was sadder than watching crippled Dickey Lovato and shriveled Sally Pacheco clop around in front of the class. It didn't do much for that day's regard for my mom and even further drained my enthusiasm for duding up for the ladies' club.

There's lots of sadness to life for sure. Everything isn't exactly tragic but sad things happen all the time. One time, after I got to know Milo a little better in class and after school when the Duncan yoyo guys came around carving parrots and flamingos and palm trees on your yoyo, new or old, he was doing some yoyo tricks like "Rock the Baby," "Walk the Dog," "Around the World" and the "Tommy Gun," he said, "Hey Rory, want to come over and see my Benjamin air rifle? It's real powerful. Shoots pellets or BB's. You can eat supper with me too."

So I finally persuaded my mom and got permission to walk over to Milo's house, there along the ditch—about a thirty-minute walk if you cut across an alfalfa field or two. I promised to call her to pick me up, insisting I had to stay for dinner or Milo might be hurt. He was a tough little guy on the surface but easily hurt and then he would pout and mope around. You could for sure tell when he got ticked off.

Anyway, I got to Milo's house, coming in from the back yard and it was pretty ugly, all kinds of stuff lying around in the dirt—hubcaps, a tire or two, empty bottles, an old, rusty American Flyer wagon. There had been a lawn, Bermuda grass or something, but it had long since died. Nothing was tended to or put in its place. It was just a real trashy place. My dad would have had a fit since he made me actually sweep our lawn after he mowed it. And when Milo invited me inside, the back porch things looked even worse, what with the screens ripped and hanging and an old couch with the stuffing popping out. But the gun was new, still in a box in oiled paper and not a scuffmark on it or speck of rust on the barrel. The stock had a couple of faint notches carved in it but all in all it was a super gun. How he afforded it was baffling. No Red Ryder Daisy toy for Milo!

"Sweet gun Milo, where'd you get it?" I asked, much impressed but a little nervous too because I could tell this was pretty much a real gun.

"Long story, Rory. My Uncle Bob somehow got it for me...said I could keep it if I took good care of it and carved a notch for every thing I killed."

So we sallied forth to try it out. I thought we'd just shoot bottles or tin cans or something, you know, target shoot. But Milo said we were going to kill some birds.

And sure enough we hadn't walked far into this stand of cottonwood and Russian olive trees and we found plenty of songbirds, finches, larks, brown thrashers, sparrows mostly, but also a mourning dove in its nest. It was a beautiful sight, what with that finely contoured rose-gray head and big dark eyes looking over the rim of its carefully crafted residence.

We got pretty close and then the dove fluttered out of its nest and started flopping around on the ground, stirring up dead leaves and little pockets of dust. I thought it was wounded at first and then I remembered my dad telling me that doves do that, go through those antics to protect their nest and distract a predator.

He was a good hunter, my dad, and I'd seen him hit a dove so high that it took minutes for it to spiral down, wings extended like a feathered helicopter. He could hit quail and pheasants and ducks when no one else could even spot them. But when Milo took aim and shot this poor protective mother dove I knew this was different. In the distance I heard a Flicker sound what seemed like a sort of mournful soul lament.

And I hadn't even tried to stop Milo! I immediately told myself I hadn't had time to save the poor creature and its young, but when he just left it there on the ground and started to walk away I finally spoke up, saying, "Why'd you do a thing like that, man? There are eggs in that nest and the mother was just trying to start a family."

"Well I don't have a mother or much of a family so what the hell of a difference does it make, Rory, if that shit happens to dumb birds? Besides, its fun."

That took me up short and I didn't say any more but was ready to go home, dreading that I had promised to eat supper with him and the family he said he didn't have. But then I got a little curious and steeled myself to see what family dinner at Milo's house meant to someone as dejected and uncaring and downright messed up as Milo.

§

When we got back to the house his family was already at the dinner table—just three people.

"You and your friend wash up, Milo, and get back here to the table quick like," came the gruff words of the man with white hair and a ruddy face seated at what seemed to be the head of the table. He was at the far end, anyway.

Then the young girl, older than Milo for sure, spoke up, "Going to all get cold. I fried the spam just the way you like it...Junior."

She was pretty enough despite quite a bit of acne, and sporting an all too short ponytail, the nubbin of hair held tight by a twisted brown rubber band. She wore a red plaid cowboy shirt with the top snaps open showing the straps of her brassiere stretched taut with the weight of her nice, mounding breasts.

The man at the other end of the table from the white-headed guy was huge, a really big man, mostly bald with a round pockmarked face and thin lips with tobacco stains lining the rim of his mouth. He didn't say much, pausing only to nod while devouring a big spam, mustard and catsup, white bread sandwich.

Milo motioned for me to follow him into the bathroom where there were old, used-up, shrunken and cracked bars of soap, half-full bottles of shampoo, Lavoris, and what not. He turned on the sink faucet and handed me a grimy bar of Lava soap. I had to use the toilet and it wasn't very appetizing to look at, what with all the yellow piss and caked shit.

"That's my Uncle Bob, the big bruiser, and my sister, Laney, and my dad. He doesn't have much to say, not since my mom died quite a while back. He was never happy though, always quarreling with mom and her yelling at him for tracking in grease and mud. Old Bob—he laughs all the time, is a big fan of Minnie Pearl and likes us to call him "Uncle Nabob" like on the Grand Ole Opry. Just wait. You'll see. Laney pretty much does the cooking and looks after things best as she can when she gets the urge or when my uncle gets after her and me. He's a real hellion and loses his temper lots. Funny thing, when he gets mad he really starts to laugh, raising his voice so the whole street can hear—so loud that C.V. Hankins, Dexter's dad across the street, comes over to check things out. Maybe it's that W.E. Garrett Snuff that Bob uses. You know, when it kicks in for him.

Dexter's mom, by the way, is one pretty woman—auburn hair, painted fingernails and toenails. Nice perfume and in the summer she wears shorts and a halter. I go over there as much as I can. My mom really blew a fuse when dad said his brother would be living with us for a time. She hated old Bob and took after him with a meat cleaver one evening about this time, right after supper—like now. Chased him around the same damn table where we're headed. Nearly cut his nuts off.

When we sat down in the two empty chairs across from Laney, Milo scraped the floor a bit with the chair and Bob started laughing and scolded Milo real good for having clumsy table manners. "Leave your manners outside? That's no way to seat yourself at the table, especially when you've invited your friend here over for a nice repast." Milo's dad just scowled at Bob but didn't say anything. Neither did Laney.

"What's your name young man?" Bob asked, turning his bowling ball head to look straight at me with what looked more like finger holes than eyes.

"Rory John Strayhope," I said with some force, refusing to be intimidated by him.

"Well, howdy, I'm just so proud to make the acquaintance of a gentleman with a name like Rory John. I do declare that's an uncommon moniker here in Grinder Switch. But it's all my pleasure I'm sure. Milo probably told you I'm his uncle Bob, but everyone calls me Uncle Nabob. That sobriquet is pretty much a power match for the likes of a name like Rory Strayhope, I'd say. I made most of my money as a wrestler, you know, and you'll have to wrestle me after supper, or just before you leave. It's up to you. But wrestle me you must. Or you can wrestle Milo in my stead. I took first place five times in Petaluma at their arm wrestling contest out there. Aunt Ambrosia, or the gal I called Ambrosia, was beaming with pride in those days, yes indeed. Ever hear of me on the airwaves or on TV? Uncle Nabob, the nattering nabob of annihilation?"

"Rory Chucklehead, we'll call you! Or better yet Sir R.J. or The Great Roar-ee of the Crowd! Down at the Armory where Mike London matched me against the likes of the Masked Marvel, Gorgeous George, and El Frijolito Salton."

"Come on Uncle Bob," Laney said, "enough of your BS. Leave the poor kid alone."

"Yeah," said Milo, "he ain't said or done nothing...but say, Uncle Bob, we killed a bird while ago. She's still there, if you wanna go see! That makes three this week, Bob. You should feel okay about that, right? I mean I'm putting the gun to good use."

"Sure Milo, but watch your smart-ass mouth or I'll have to box those big cauliflower ears of yours again. Make them drain your brains. That would cheer me up right nice."

Milo asked his dad to pass the potatoes and peas and he scooped out a big spoonful, shoveling it into his mouth before he had time to pass it on to me. Laney offered me half of a spam sandwich with one mustard-globbed heel, and said, " We were out of Vienna Sausages but this fried spam here ain't so bad. I fried it in some choice lard and the mustard makes it pussy-cat tasty."

Even before the first bite I knew the cat food, or whatever they called it, was no good, just skimpy grub to start with and no flavor to anything. Peanut butter and jelly would have beat fried spam. It was nothing like the wilted lettuce, onion, and radish salad that would be on the table at home—complete with a nice bacon and tomato sandwich on Rainbow bread swathed in Miracle Whip—with fresh green onions! But I was polite, stayed true to my manners and swallowed most everything with feigned appetite and praise.

There was nothing to drink but water and it was warm—no ice or refrigerator chill. It doesn't take any economic smarts to tell this was not a well-off family: cheap clothes, cheap furniture, cheap food, and bad manners all around—no one really trying to put a best foot forward entertaining me. What did I expect, you say? Well, friendship coats over lots of things.

Milo and I smiled at each other and then at Laney, and old Bob and his brother started grumbling about politics and this horse's ass president and that S.O.B mayor and what a bastard so and so was and all I hear is a barrage of cuss words flying over and across the table. I tuned it out until

Laney piped up and said, "Holy Shit, can't you two geezers shut the fuck up? Milo's got company, for Christ sakes!" And she picks up her dirty plate, clanging the silverware together, and heads for the kitchen, shaking her head while I stare at her round, nicely undulating rear end.

Then Milo asks if we could be excused and starts to leave the table but Uncle Bob grabs him by the arm and slaps him really hard along side the face, the same side as his bad ear. And he lets out a wail and starts to cry and Bob yells out, "I warned you, you little prick, to mind your manners, you and your smart ass uppity little pissant buddy here.

Just then, Laney stormed back from the kitchen and starts to pound on Bob's shoulder, screaming for him to let Milo go. Which he does but before I know what's going on Bob shoots up from his chair, grabs Laney in a bear hug, and carries her into the living room and slams her down on the old moth-eaten couch, Then he straddles her skinny legs with his giant porker loins and sits down on her squirming body.

Milo says, "Come on Rory, we got to help Laney!" And I turn to Mr. Mackey with a look of desperate dumb disbelief, wanting him to do something but he just waves me off, lights a cigarette, gets up and walks outside, ambling west, back through the trashy yard, toward the trees where Milo shot the dove.

In a flash Milo is on the couch pulling at Bob's ears and now the fat man is laughing up a storm and in a flash has both Milo and his sister pinned on the floor. "Got my dander up now. No tickling allowed I told you. I'll make you all cry Uncle Nabob before I'm through. But I'll let you go if little 'Sir Lion's Roary the Last' can pull me off ya both!"

"Tag team, Rory! He wants to play tag team! You got to help us!" And Milo and Laney are either crying or laughing, I don't know which—maybe more laughing than crying. So I head over and jump on Uncle Bob's back, like trying to mount a fat, wiry-haired wild boar, and he rears up like Super Pig and I fly across the room, hitting a decrepit old armchair.

"That'll teach you upstarts to horse around with Uncle Nabob, cause I damn well know how to wrestle." Then he gets off Milo and his sister and although I'm still kind of groggy I swear Bob cups one hand around both of Laney's breasts and lays his big fat fingers on her crotch—and she kind of swoons, either in pain or pleasure, I just couldn't tell.

Then she gets up, runs her hand through her hair, straightens her cowboy shirt and announces she has to fold clothes in the bedroom. I see there's a stack of rumpled clothes on the unmade bed across the hall and she's in there in a couple of three strides with Uncle Bob right behind her, and him saying, "You two bums shut the crap up and watch the T.V. while I help Laney with her clothes."

And while I'm trying to clear my head and Milo's rubbing his ear he turns on the Philco television with a rainbow decal over the screen to make it seem like a color picture. Then he turns up the volume but I can still hear scuffling and groaning and moaning—and what sounds like laughter. And it's not just Milton Berle and the men from Texaco, working from Maine to Mexico. It's coming from behind the closed bedroom door where all those rumpled clothes were.

§

It was dusk and I told Milo I had to get home and, neglecting to call for a ride like I promised, I walked pretty fast to get there. I couldn't tell whether it was the deepening darkness, my banged head, or the wind in my face that caused everything to look blurry. All I knew was that I was scared and I kept seeing that poor dove fluttering around on the leaf strewn ground, hearing its wings flap in mournful applause to the accompaniment of that distant tragic Flicker's song mingling with the wind, the whimpering of Laney, and the grunts of Uncle Bob coming from behind that closed bedroom door. And there in the jumble of all those clothes piled atop the unmade bed, where all of my thoughts and images were flooding my naïve but awakened boyish mind—there, in the hubbub of all that I still heard Laney's shirt snaps pop open in a barrage that sounded like my dad banging away at doves with his Winchester automatic shotgun.

Anyway, I made it home down ditches and across alfalfa fields and down dusky streets to the sanctuary of my home shining bright through the encroaching night. My mother asked some worried questions but I just said "I met Milo's dad, Mr. Mackey, and his brother, Uncle Bob, and Milo's sister, Laney, and that she fixed a fine supper and then we all arm wrestled Uncle Bob, who used to be a champion wrestler called Uncle Nabob in California, and that he made us all holler 'Uncle' pretty darn fast. Then Milo and I watched some fake color TV show about these men from Texaco dressed up in caps and bow ties, sort of like Dad wore at the station and when that was over I walked home."

I didn't dare tell her all about what I really saw and how scary and downright ugly and mean old Uncle Bob was. Or even that he still liked to be called by his wrestling name, Uncle Nabob, for some dumb reason and made fun of my name as being fancy but not as fancy as his or Milo's and how they kept calling me "Sir This and Sir That," and Milo "Junior" because Milo was his father's name too. But they didn't call him Senior, just Mac or Mackey.

All the while it was Laney I kept thinking about and how she looked when Uncle Bob put his hand on her crotch and over her breasts and how I would like to do the same darn thing and see her unsnap her shirt like a string of Chinese fire crackers, and toss it on that unmade bed and "un-maiden" her like Larry Gallegos told me about when he'd seen his parents wrestling around on the floor without any clothes on in front of a Christmas fireplace. He told me you had to get on top of each other some how to really do it.

§

I saw Milo at school for a couple of weeks, doing yoyos and playing tops or marbles. He was an expert at both games, had a beautiful green and red Tennessee Walker top as well as a couple of vicious Saint Louis Spikes. He had a great collection of marbles, especially shooters—plus a cloth bag of agate boulders and select steelies. Milo always played for keeps and never allowed anyone to fudge when shooting. He could clean out the pot in a matter of minutes.

We never talked much about that supper at this house though he did show me a couple of new wrestling holds Uncle Bob taught him. And, dumb, I consented to be shown, knowing that if they were Bob's techniques they were sure to hurt. So one recess, just after cleaning the pot and destroying Troy Abrams in a marble game where Milo added another dozen marbles to his collection, he asked, "Say, Rory, do you know how to milk a mouse or how a turkey jumps over a log?" I didn't, of course, and immediately wished I hadn't consented to be shown.

His fingers were chapped and caked with dust and dirt and I watched and writhed in pain as he took my little finger and bent it back on itself offering me the out of saying "Uncle," which I did plenty quick. During that moment of recovery he reached up and pulled the short hairs on the back of my neck and jerked hard as he could while gobbling like a damn turkey and chanting "Turkey, turkey from Albuquerque. Turkey, turkey from Albuquerque." I tried to tough it out but I was tearing up in spite of myself while Milo laughed just like Uncle Nabob—a happy but mean kind of laugh, one that the Devil himself might devise.

§

I steered clear of Milo for a time after that. Being Milo's friend had too many upsetting consequences and I should have known better too when he invited me to a picnic at Coyote Canyon in the Manzano Mountains. He said it would be fun and it was being sponsored by the Army Corps of Engineers and that his dad and uncle had worked for them out at Manzano Base—something to do with building bunkers and storing bombs.

Milo built it all up telling about how there would be volleyball games and lots of food and soda pop and there was this one girl, a friend of Laney's, he knew would be coming and that she was "stacked like a shit house," or something like that. He called her "Ginger Snapper" and said he would explain all that later.

Who could resist an invitation like that, especially if you were tired of being well behaved and good and all that when Milo's world was so trashy? It took some convincing but I assured my overprotective mom that Mr. Mackey would drive and that it would just be a short distance away in the mountains. She, of course, knew picnic areas in the mountains and had been on a picnic or two in the Manzanos herself with dad. And I'd even been up to Doc Long's nestled just off the main highway in the coolness of pine trees, a popular get away spot in the Sandias with plenty of tables and fire pits for roasting weiners and toasting marshmallows.

Like most everyone, she had no idea who Doc Long was, or just where Coyote Canyon was located, or when the Sandia Mountains became the Manzano Mountains or which highway was which. But I told her that the picnic was sponsored by the Army Corps of Engineers, so what could go wrong?

Anyway, that convinced her and I got to go. So Mr. Mackey, Milo, and Uncle Bob picked me up in an old Chevrolet pea-green panel truck with the word "Deliveries" and a faded phone number painted on the side. It was a tight squeeze crawling over Bob to get where Milo was in the tattered old back seat. Bob smelled like snuff and sweat and needed a bath. He wore the same old snuff-stained coveralls but had on a new looking red plaid shirt. When he greeted me with "Welcome aboard Sir Squirt!" the stench of his breath and his B.O. just about knocked me back into the driveway. Mr. Mackey just said "Hello, son," and we were off in a black cloud of exhaust smoke.

Milo was seated near some cases of Schlitz and a couple of volleyballs were rolling around behind the beer, confined to a small space by nets and poles.

"Ready to play ball, Squirt? Nothing like beer and balls I always say if you know what I mean. I never go anywhere without my balls? Say, you know what the tall guy said to the midget at the other end of the bar don't you?" Bob asked me and started laughing in the middle of the question.

"Nope, can't say that I do," I replied to the sound of Milo groaning "Don't fall for his dumb jokes, Rory!"

"You shut the Schlitz up Milo," old Bob said reaching back to try and ear-swat his nephew. "I'll tell you if you don't know, 'Burpster.' The tall guy at the bar said to the midget at the bar, 'Hey peewee, the highballs are on me!' Get it, get it?" And then he roared with laughter and let go out the window with a big glob of brownish-black spit. "The high balls are on old Uncle Nabob and don't you forget it...want a pinch of gun powder between your cheek and gum and I mean your face cheek not your ass cheeks. Or maybe a chaw of Tonto's tobacco?"

"No thanks, Uncle Bob," I said with a mock little boy smile and we traveled on, taking the curves though Tijeras canyon, past the Paradise Club tucked near a spring and grove of trees on old Highway 66, there where the two ranges of mountains scissor together, the Sandias to the north and the Manzanos to the south...with both Milo and me leaning forward to hear Mr. Mackey and Bob hold forth, reminiscing about their work with atomic bombs.

I thought it was pretty much bullshit but Milo assured me he'd seen their ID cards giving them clearance to Sandia Base. I wondered if I could possibly confirm it by asking to see those IDs but Milo waved me off, saying, "Just listen...you don't often hear my dad talk about it but Bob, well he's a blowhard and doesn't know what 'classified information' means."

The boulders were big and jagged-high, and dangerously balanced on both sides of the canyon walls. I tried to stick my heard forward to get as much fresh air as I could for my queasy stomach what with the claustrophobic feeling I was getting in the back seat, and with exhaust fumes coming through the floor boards. That's one big disadvantage of a panel truck. No windows for the passengers in back. Surely the cases of beer we were transporting to the picnic didn't need the fresh air like I did. But I tuned in again to the brothers talking about their exploits.

"Remember that night at the Paradise Club when that red headed stripper was doing her thing...one tit going clockwise and the other counter clockwise? I mean, Mac, that's the most fun I've ever seen you have? You know don't you that old Dick Bills' nephew has gone and made it big with his chicken-pickin' guitar licks. And not just playing in strip joints either?"

"Well, how about the time we stopped along the side of the road on reservation land to enjoy a couple of cold brews, waiting for the dust to settle from all the tractors and bulldozers, and that damn blackbear straight out of Hell Canyon decided to run down the mountain like some wild, horny Injun squaw who took a sudden to liking to us? Watching your fat ass running back to the truck was more fun than that gal's talented tits!"

"I wasn't scared...just smart let's say. Not as scared as you when you tried to out run that dynamite blast when you ran out of time and drilled your detonation holes too short for a good fit and that brain at the trigger box nearly killed us? Your fault or his wasn't even in question...just that we survived."

Milo leaned over close to my ear and said, "I knew I should have brought my air rifle. I guess there are lots of bears up here—and coyotes too, and probably the ghosts of a couple of dead Indians and some radioactive scientists. That's how all these canyons got their names you know."

§

What I did know was that lots of military planes flew in and out of Kirtland and Manzano Base. I'd been to some air shows on the base and even saw a B-36 up close one time and a couple of B-47's along with a B-57 or two and I'd heard talk about the atomic bomb stockpile in the mountains. My dad bemoaned it, echoing Ike's "military industrial complex," but the economy, and maybe the destiny of the city, depended on the local government workforce. I'd heard some talk about where the bomb was first exploded at Trinity Site, and about the uranium mines over by Grants where one of our cousins lived, and secret missile and jet research labs down around Alamogordo and White Sands. They said they used monkeys to test all that. And maybe it was related to the space aliens and Martians who landed in nearby Roswell. So all this bomb talk wasn't new. It was just that Uncle Bob and Mr. Mackey apparently helped dynamite all the holes in the hills. I was starting to daydream about it all, seeing the mountains explode and a mushroom cloud covering the city, when I tuned back in to hear Uncle Nabob say, "I wonder how many bombs they have now in those caves we helped dynamite out of ancient rock? They could blow the whole damn city to smithereens, and everything else between Los Alamos and Stallion's Gate. Better say your prayers to the Father, Son, and Holy Ghost. I told you that I actually saw the light from that first blast when I was working construction in Moriarty and Vaughn."

§

I was getting pretty car sick again, but after more hairpin turns going up the mountain we saw a lot of parked cars and people carrying baskets and boxes of food and drinks and we were finally there, announced too by a large roughly-hewn brown State Highway sign with gold letters, "Coyote Canyon."

Bob ordered Milo and me to unload the cases of beer and carry them over to a table where a blonde young woman was waiting, motioning us to hurry up. Turns out it was this Ginger gal, Laney's friend. And Milo wasn't exaggerating when he said she was curvy. Made your eyes snap—which I guess is what Milo meant by her name. Her face wasn't all that great—big featured I guess you'd say, full lips, large horse-like teeth, and lots of them you could see, and I almost gave up counting when she smiled. Man, she had a body like a movie star—unlike that of even the prettiest girls I'd seen at Tingley Beach. And my imagination kept telling me just how great she'd look in one of those two-piece suits. Laney introduced us and Ginger captured my heart when she reached down and pinched my cheek, saying what a cute kid I was. She wasn't wearing a bra either! I just wished I wasn't a kid or that she didn't see me as such. But I was glad I hadn't taken Uncle Bob's offer of a little pinch between the cheek and gum.

Bob and Mr. Mackey disappeared into the crowd, shaking some hands and going over where the hamburgers and hotdogs were cooking. And after helping set up a couple of volleyball nets we picked up a couple of drinks—Orange Crush for me and Royal Crown for Milo. And as we sat at a picnic table with all kinds of names and hearts and arrows carved in the food-stained top Milo proposed we go exploring and look for the bomb caves. "What about bears?" I asked.

Are you a dirty dog coward? He asked and before I could finish disputing him he was heading up a little pine-stippled canyon and me right behind him. We climbed some boulders, throwing our pop bottles in the air just to see where they would fall and splatter. "Bombs away!" Milo yelled and I cheered loudest since my bottle broke into more pieces. "Orange Crushed! Milo, what did you expect?" We kept going, horsing around, following a mountain blue jay, watching some vultures soar overhead high on thermals, tossing rocks just to hear them clatter—and then Milo stopped up short and bent down to dig away some lichen-covered stones from a little glint of silver.

"Look at this, a pocket knife, and a neat one. It's a three-bladed Buck with the black handle barely scratched." He worked the blades in and out a few times to get the dirt out and then let me hold it and examine it. There was very little rust but you could tell it had been there quite some time, caked in dirt as it was.

"I'll bet the bomb workmen dropped it and we're getting pretty close."

We might have been close to the restricted area and the top-secret bomb bunkers but we were pretty far away from the picnic grounds. No sounds except for some jet very high above us.

"Kinda lost, I guess," Milo said, looking up at the jet. I think we should go back the way we came."

But we were both really turned around so I said we should find a fence line and then walk down it. That's what "Argosy" and "True" and all the men's magazines said to do.

What fence line, Rory? Do you see a damn fence line? Show me a fuckin' fence line and I'll walk down it with you.

Then we heard a noise...maybe a coyote, or a bear snort or a mountain lion yawn or something. There were grunts and moans and some loud laughter so we followed the sounds only to see, surprise of surprises, old Uncle Nabob with his coveralls down around his ankles and his ugly white ass pointing up to the con-trails of that long gone jet. He was bent over a good-sized boulder pumping away at some heavy-breasted, naked girl who was saying, "Oh, hey, oh hey, okay, okay!"

"Yea, Yea! Say it, got to say Uncle, say it, Uncle...Nay...Bob! Uncle Yea Bob!"

We stared hard. Real hard—Milo and me, our eyes making popping sounds like Laney's shirt snaps, then wet, squishy noises when we rubbed our eyes, and wiped our saliva lips, wet with excitement.

"Who's the girl he's doing it to? Is it Ginger? I whispered to Milo. "I can't see her face or her clothes or anything other than...."

I think, I think...we'd better get the hell out of here before Uncle Bob sees us. When he laughs that much he can be really, really mad."

"Howdy, howdy, howdy, howdy, "I'm just so glad to do you!" I heard Bob grunt out seemingly to Milo and me, as we ran back down to a new awareness of just what it meant to be a nabob like Uncle Bob.

Was it pleasure or pain? Was the object of his affection Ginger, or someone else? Someone younger? Someone older? Somehow I knew it was neither and it was both. It was one and it was all. In that lasting boyhood mystery I see her still spread out over that smooth sun-hot boulder crying " Oh, Uncle Nabob," amidst the snorts and laughter. I say it myself at times when it seems the only thing to say, when I love so much it hurts. When I laugh so hard I cry "Uncle! Uncle Nabob! Uncle Nabob!"

Lucinda and the Wild Birds

"When I found a flicker feather caught between the fingers of sage, its burned red shaft spoke to the bravery of this bird who flew directly toward the sun to retrieve fire for the people."
—Terry Tempest Williams, *When Women Were Birds*

Lucinda comes to me in my dreams, and I don't know what to make of her visits. Those dreams come almost every night now. It's a sure thing if I go out to the chicken coop roof to look at the stars. She comes to me in daydreams as well, and I often can't tell the daydreams from the night dreams. Sometimes her goats come with her. Sometimes she comes surrounded by flocks of birds. Sometimes she comes alone.

I saw her almost every day, especially in spring and summer when I walked the edges of the big alfalfa field behind my house looking for wild asparagus and dill, and watching the wild birds...all kinds of beautiful birds, although the flickers or yellowhammers are my favorite bird, both in the way they look and fly, and in their song: just a single note, loud, piercing, fast and then long diminishing. And their feathers, their plumage is so varied, solid colors, yet speckled patterns, red accents, yet white too—astonishingly beautiful.

Their flight is similar to their song too, a climb, then a dip down, and then another climb followed by that looping, downward dip. Usually they sing, or maybe it's better to say they whistle, when ground feeding, or clinging to the trunk of an ash, an elm, or a cottonwood tree. It's a forlorn song, not as sad as a dove's or a whippoorwill's, but single half or whole notes—a melancholy lament. No chirping or chattering for flickers. Their tap, tap, tap pecking is in a contrasting staccato pattern to their song, as if they keep time while they sing or between songs. But they don't always tap on wood! Sometimes they tap at a tin roof or piece of scrap metal. How could such a thing be? Such coordinated adaptation—feathers, song, flight, pecking. Wondrous winged ways!

What a striking contrast of sounds compared to the harsh, grating, bleating of Lucinda's goats, or, I should say Chano's, her father's, goats. He's retired from the Santa Fe Railroad and raises goats to boost his pension. Lucinda says she gets little or no money for her work as his goat herder. It's as if she owes it to Chano and her mother, Elena—as beautiful a woman as Chano is ugly.

Chano raised dairy goats, sold goat milk, and even, sorrowful to say, butchered them, usually the cabróncitos, the kids, and sold the meat for chile and other recipes that call for goat meat, or in the case of tripe, goat guts. His back yard was one big goat pen, cobbled together out of salvaged, rust-colored lumber from the railroad yard.

I don't like goat meat or the milk, or even the goats, though I know that each goat has a separate personality, or seems to. My sisters drink goat's milk and treat their hair with it too. But then, they do other strange things like put hot wax on their face, let it dry, and then pull it off fast with a yelp! Always followed by soothing, pleasurably painful astringent slaps. My father says goat meat is tasty fried with mountain oysters, which I don't' care for either. They make good breakfasts, he says. It surely pains me to see him devour them.

So although I don't care for goats or their meat, I do like Lucinda, her beautiful face, soft voice, and her cruel but mostly loving ways. Una mujer muy, muy bonita!

§

I first saw Lucinda face-to-face one day in spring when I was out with my father helping clean the irrigation ditches, preparing for opening the gates from the Acequia Madre or mother ditch which feeds our small ditch. The small ditch ran behind Lucinda's house, on its way past the Vigil acreage, next to our place, and then on down to a few other farms that also have gardens and pastures and some animals—maybe a cow, a horse or two, hogs, chickens, cats, and, of course, dogs. My mother raised dogs, by the way, and she could dock their tails: one, two, three!

I had seen Lucinda from a distance and thought of her as the "goat girl" since she always had two or three goats following her around or she was following them, never a herd but usually a doe and kids. The old buck stayed pretty close to home. Lucinda said he was a Nubian goat and much prized by Chano; but more about that Nubian pendejo later.

On that particular face off day I was a good fifty or seventy-five yards from my dad who was at the main ditch gate, talking to Chano, an angular, boney man, and I was raking and hoeing and pitching brush and dead grass and scraps of paper, a whisky or wine bottle or two, and some bottles—the usual accumulation of seasonal trash. Once in a while I'd find a used rubber, all yellow-white and wrinkled and twisted back on itself. Sometimes it would be bloody, suggesting more pain than pleasure, though I didn't really know that much at the time about such things.

I turned around to pitch a bunch of weeds over my shoulder up onto the ditch bank—and there, amidst the sound of tinkling bells and the muffled but still audible chomping and chewing of goats was this pretty girl.

Then the words, "Qué tal? I'm Lucinda, and you?"

"Lucinda you say, or Luciana? I asked in a stutter.

"Either one. I like both names. Luciana is the softer me. Lucinda is my tougher self."

"Okay, claro. Rory, Rory John Strayhope's my name—but you can call me R.J. if you like. Vivo dos casas a la sur. Mucho gusto en conocer la."

"You're hard at work on your Spanish I see but I think I'll just call you Rory. I try to let my goats do my ditch clearing work for me...easy as thumbing through the yellow pages—which they would also eat if they got the chance. Paper, thistles, wrappers, they'll eat anything and chomp and cough while doing it."

"Lucky you," I said, "Will they eat rubber too?" I asked, out of veiled mischief.

"Sometimes I guess. I don't watch them all the time. No tires or anything, though."

Then, changing the subject fast I asked, "Isn't that your father talking to my father at the irrigation gate? They talk, the goats work, and we watch?"

"Oh, I'm working too. Taking care of goats isn't as easy as it looks. They can roam too far and get themselves and me in trouble fast."

"Are they your pets?" I asked her, noticing that she dressed something like our housekeeper, dear old Satherine. Lucinda's shoes were ankle high, thick soled, and scuffed—much in need of oiling. Her thick stockings, almost puttees, covered her calves and looked hot and uncomfortable, stippled as they were with cockleburs, a few stickers, some of them, ironically the common local stickers called "goat heads."

"Oh, no, well, in a way. We sell their milk and sometimes them. So they're my father's, my family's business, although I'm told to take care of them, be responsible for them. I love them and I hate them if that makes any sense, stubborn but endearing at the same time—ugly as demons, yet pretty as angels, maybe like me. Do you like goat's milk? It's healthy and for some women even a beauty aid—good for your hair and complexion too, they say.

"Nope, never liked it but I've heard about how it's good for the face and hair and all, and for temperamental stomachs."

I couldn't help but notice, however, that Lucinda's face, her complexion wasn't the best, kind of pimply like mine, especially around the edges of her nose where little beads of perspiration held on. Otherwise, her skin was clear (although she did have thin, fine black hair forming barely perceptible sideburns spreading into her rounded cheekbones). But the little red eruptions did no real harm to her beauty...and before I caught myself I blurted out, "You use it yourself, do you?"

"Me, oh, sometimes, I've tried it but I can't break into family profit too often by indulging myself in beauty routines. My older sister, Irene, uses it regularly but she's the beauty of the family. She works downtown at Kistler-Collister in foundations and waits on all the country club women. Anyway...oh look, look up there...the sky...it's a sharp-shinned hawk I believe, buscando por ratones, lagartijas, uno pajarito, o una culebra."

It was a beautiful hawk, soaring in wide circles in the blue, cloudless sky, but still close enough you could see its coloring and its wing and tail shape. I didn't know its scientific name but had seen larger ones around our chicken coop. I recognized the screeching cry I'd heard in the dark outside my bedroom window. Suddenly it took a steep dive, capturing a rather large mouse and carrying it into a cottonwood tree over by the main ditch not far from our fathers. It started tearing apart the mouse immediately, pulling at long strings of intestine.

"Mira! They don't even notice the death drama in front of them, always talking business and politics and Conservancy irrigation calendars, workmen, and water policies.

"You know your birds," I said. "Can you identify most of them? I like the flicker and other woodpeckers like the ladder back best. But I admire the brown thrasher too. They stick by their thistle or cactus nests until doomsday. How about you?"

"I like Mexican sparrows, house finches really, and their singing—like a Mexican canary warbling."

"You mean the sparrows with the red-tinged head and breast?"

"Seguro, ugly beauty, plain beauty, with a virtuoso song that few other birds around here can match. And, yes I can identify most birds since I spend lots of time watching wild birds while out with my goats. Bird songs, bird music I call it, tells me many things—about the weather, about the seasons, about what's stirring them up, or if they're relaxed and just singing their special songs. Birds just sing. Whether they know what they're singing about doesn't matter. They just sing. No such thing as birdbrains! Birds are smart and teach us lots if we just notice them. You'll have to watch and listen to them with me sometime. We can wander with the goats and the birds and just talk about nature and the trees and fields. Maybe we'll spot your beloved flicker, also called a yellowhammer you know."

"Yes, but why that name, or even flicker for that matter? Who named them, anyway? Maybe Audubon?"

"No se, I don't know. Ornithologists, quizas."

§

And that's how our friendship started, Lucinda and me, and how that very night I started dreaming about her and thinking about her and her goats and wild birds. I even dreamed of birds sitting on her shoulder and on the backs and the heads of her goats like those paintings of Adam and Eve at peace in the Garden of Eden.

Soon we were taking long walks together, or sitting under the shade of a cottonwood tree by the alfalfa field, or finding asparagus stalks together and chewing on them raw, like her goats eating grass. We'd stop by her house and put the goats up, and then we'd walk down to my house and climb up on the chicken coop, using the big stinkwood trees as ladders, and we'd just lie there looking at the deep sky, or watching the sun set on the mountains, turning them watermelon pink. We'd try seeing birds and animals in cloud shapes and try to stay out to watch the moon, big and golden, rise over the mountains. It was on the roof of the chicken coop one time at dusk she first kissed me—sending such new feelings through me I thought I was some flying, enchanted, wild bird.

§

Sometimes Lavola, my mother, would ask me to bring her a big hen from the chicken coop. I hated to go into the chicken pen since it wasn't the cleanest place, what with all the droppings of caca de gallina, chicken shit, but I had to chase down whatever chicken my mother wanted. My father avoided the place like the bubonic plague since he had really bad lung problems, allergies, yes, but he had also recovered from tuberculosis and always relied on our sympathies for what he advertised as his weak lungs. "That will damn sure choke me up!" he'd say about lots of things, and not just the chicken coop.

I was usually the one to collect the eggs for whatever meal or recipe and that was worth it because there was nothing better than a supper of scrambled eggs and green Hatch chile—two "hatches," we'd joke, for one sort of thing—Hatch being a renowned chile capitol, and eggs that had been "hatched," a funny enough idea. But what I dreaded most was being chased by one of the meanest roosters around.... We named him Floyd after Pretty Boy Floyd. He was a large Rhode Island Red, with an oversized crimson, seemingly cultivated comb, and a gangster's personality. He would rush at me, just like Lucinda's pendejo ram, El Cabrón, and try to spur me and peck me—it called for unnatural athletic ability to evade the gruesome guy.

If I could evade the chicken shit and Floyd's meanness and chase down the right plucky Wyandotte hen I felt lucky—until I handed the poor victim over to my mother who grabbed it in a tight grip and swung it in one high arc after another, wringing its neck until its head came off. Then the pitiful hen ran around the yard, heading, headless, it knew not where, over the little ditch bridge and into the rose garden, under the fruit trees, out into the vegetable garden, squirting geysers of blood, and eventually collapsing, flapping its useless wings, like a distressed mother dove, in a row of protruding radishes, made all the more red by the hen's spurts of blood. You don't ever want to see that if you have any feelings for chickens or any other kind of bird. Better to be a wild bird and face the hands of fate, I thought, rather than to suffer a pioneer neck ringing. Even old Floyd, mean as he was, deserved a better fate than a randomly chosen hen when it came to mother's strong-talented arm swings and wrist twists.

§

Speaking of fate, one evening when Lucinda and I were talking about how mean Floyd was and how life in the chicken coop wasn't all that great, what with the pecking order and all the bullying for control and how that's how some men got the name of being "henpecked," and how some people were said to be "cocksure," or a "cock of the walk," and how size wasn't the main factor, in that bantam roosters were sometimes just as aggressive as a big rooster.

"And how about the other rooster word, you know, 'cock'?" Lucinda asked straight away. And then, surprise of all surprises she proceeded to talk about other kinds of things and show me what it meant beyond just words. We'd known each other in our talks for some time. And she'd visited me in my dreams lots but never like this. Maybe it was just a night dream, but one I kept dwelling on time and again even in mid-day when we were together walking the fields and pastures.

No sooner was that one evening's surprise lesson over than out of the descending darkness down swept the largest hawk ever imagined, big as a damn eagle, a giant bird looking almost prehistoric, and like my mother eyeballing the hens, it zeroed in on its chosen chicken. But just as its talons were about to hit the target, Floyd darts over and the feathers fly—chicken feathers, hawk feathers, rooster feathers—but the giant Pterodactyl-like bird wins and carries Floyd away high into the thickening darkness. Only poor Floyd's prodigious, castrated and forlorn comb remained amidst the dust and shit on the ground. Lucinda and I were speechless for the longest time, sitting there next to each other. "Did you ever imagine such an awful thing happening, Lucinda, did you?"

"It's the way of the world, a ghost hawk comes, and even the strong meet their match and, it's over. Demons or maybe angels of death of one kind or another are always the victors. Atrapado en el tiempo. Rodeado por los demonios y sin esperanza! Better to make love than talk about fate and demons."

What began as dichos became dreams, or what began as a reverie tuned into kisses. It's hard for me to tell any more. Can you think or talk things into becoming or do they become only when told or talked about? A kiss isn't just a kiss, regardless.

Lucinda wasn't the only companion I had. One fateful day in April, Milo Mackey came over and he brought his air rifle with him. He had a lingering meanness about him and liked to shoot birds and rabbits and dogs, and just about anything that moved. I'd experienced that first hand but, still trying to remain friends, I invited him to gather asparagus with me and we sallied forth into the alfalfa field behind my house, heading over to the Acequia Madre.

When we met up with Lucinda, Milo started joking that he would like to see what her goats would do if he shot one in the haunches with a BB.

"That will never, never happen, lambion!" Lucinda flared. "So go shoot muskrats or something over by the ditch, but don't shoot anything around me."

As destiny would have it a beautiful flicker flew into an elm tree not far from us and before anyone could say anything or wave him off, mean Milo pumped up his gun to maximum pressure, turned fast and aimed at the flicker. It was a far distance, maybe twenty-five yards, but amazingly he hit the bird and we stood there watching it lose its grip and fall to the ground, bouncing heavily through some limbs.

Lucinda and I stood there seething while Milo ran over and retrieved the bird and brought it back to us bragging that he had hit it clean through the eye. And that's where the blood was oozing out, through the poor beautiful bird's eye. I had never seen a flicker that close and it was strangely even more beautiful than I had imagined, and yet it was grotesque—still and lifeless, its fiery feathers still vibrant despite Milo's perversion to kill it and luck allowing him to make the shot.

I carefully took the bird and dug a grave for it with a nearby tree branch, and covered it reverently with dirt, giving a little whistle imitating its call. I had heard a flicker's voice many times before. Lucinda began to cry and took her tethered goats away and in their bleating they too seemed to be mourning such a profane act, such a senseless deed that deprived even them of a fellow creature.

I went back to the house knowing that my friendship with Milo was finally over and that I would never visit him or have him visit me again for he had once before shown his true colors when he had killed a nesting dove. Even then I knew it wasn't a fluke. My remorse was great and I regretted that I had ever met him and that in fact now I not Milo had killed the one bird, the special bird, I most admired.

§

Not long after that and because of that killing, another truly tragic event occurred. We had found a nest of small birds in some low willow branches and Lucinda identified them as her favorite birds—Mexican sparrows. We watched them for several days, waiting for them to develop as fledglings and then boldly take to the sky.

One day while walking alone I came to the spot and the little birds were gone, not just the four or five baby birds but the entire nest. Panic struck me and I rushed to Lucinda's house only to find her sitting down beside the family outhouse, staring at her penned goats and a recently butchered kid hanging from the large ash tree in their yard. Her father's knives were still on the nearby table and the ground was soaked with blood. Flies were dancing on the meat.

Lucinda was absent mindedly rubbing her arms, and spitting now and then into the dirt, shaking her head and drawing lines in the sand with a blood-caked stick.

"Lucinda, the nest, the little wild birds, they're gone! Did you know? What could have happened to them? There's no wind...maybe a cat got them?"

"No, not a cat, not your mean friend," and she slowly lifted her head and nodded over to the mouth-chomping ram. "I fed some of them to El Cabrón and threw the others into the stinking cavern of the outhouse. Better to meet a cruel death young by my caring hands than have to linger. Let their mother and father bird mourn them and us—and spit in the eye of the likes of your fiendish carnal."

And all I could say and still say in my dreams is "Chingada, Lucinda! Te amo."

House Call

"In the name of Jesus Christ of Nazareth rise up and walk."
   —Acts 3:6, *The Bible*

I'd just come in from riding Jack, my stubborn donkey, a real dumb donkey if there ever was one. "Muy tonto, in Spanish!" Every time I'd ride that damn donkey at some point in the ride he would decide to take a nap and lie down in the middle of wherever we were and I'd have to jump off fast or else. It isn't as if he didn't give notice. This time he caught my foot and bit my arm! He'd start to slow his pace—not that he ever moved very fast. But the old guy could trot and we'd build up some speed now and then when I could coax him along, thanks to the poplar switch I used as a riding quirt.

When I finally reached the house, I limped in as fast as I could, barely noticing the car in the driveway, what with my whining and Jack's braying, me hopping on my right foot, and holding my poor arm, yelling out, "Old Jack, damn that dumb old Jack. He got me good this time! Mom! Satherine! Anybody! What should I do? Oh what in sweet Jesus' name should I do?" I was putting on quite a show.

Satherine heard me first: "Pobrecito, Rory John, con prisa, let Satherine help!" Seems like Satherine was always there, a housekeeper, a nurse for me, and a lady in waiting for my mother who adored her—as did I. Only father held her at some distance, saying she was kind of strange—enchanted or possessed, an opinion mother scoffed at, saying, "She's a dear, dear old woman who makes my life much easier."

"Que burro, que tonto! Cabróncito Jack!" Satherine chimed in taking my side as usual.

"Gracias, querida vieja, donde esta mamá?"

"Dentro en la sala con un hombre, pero esperate, muchacho."

Satherine said she would prepare a poultice and would talk to the donkey, scolding him into an apology. She was always telling me stories of her encounters with duende. It was a constant theme. But like duende the stories took various twists and turns.

"It's duende at work again, Rory. He plants bad ideas in Jack. Duende, El Jugador, is always playing tricks. I'll get to the bottom of his plan and teach Jack to know better how to deal with such tricksters. Duende isn't all bad, just full of mischief, and Jack's not smart enough to tell a good chiste from a bad one."

Satherine had a special way with animals and talked back and forth with them all the time, whether gathering eggs, milking the cow, calling the cats, you name it. She was from Chihuahua, and always wore a long black dress, a black cotton blouse and a black silk headscarf. Her face had canyons of wrinkles and when she brought her small, boney hand over her eyes and then down around her face you could actually see her fingers dip into those wrinkles, in and out, up and over, like a car taking the "kiss me quick" hills out on Juan Tabo road at the base of the mountains. Talk about the Hispanic sense of the sadness of life, dear Satherine always appeared to be in mourning, even when she smiled her most loving smile, showing her stained teeth worn down to the dentin. She preferred to call me Rory John or, at times, RJ—which I rather liked.

This time what damn Jack and his duende had done was lie down again without warning and while I was daydreaming about Nita Ann Turner, and how neat she looked in those symmetrically pleated, starched Levi's she always wore and how round and curvaceous her bottom was—filling out those pants like she was poured into them like pudding—and thinking to myself, "No sir,—nothing baggy about Nita's neat little ass, not like the ass I was riding or that old snuff-stained bastard Uncle Nabob Mackey," who gave me nightmares thinking about the time I saw his ugly plumber's butt when he was giving it to that girl over that huge boulder up in the mountains.

Well, about this time in the daydream old Jack decided to call it quits for his and duende's part in the ride and he decides to take a siesta in the middle of Sunset Road. And before I could pull up my mental and real pants, my poor scrawny ankle was under my donkey's big belly and I'm stuck, swatting away at Jack's haunches, stirring up dust from his bristly hair and the road and crying out my own version of "Uncle Nabob!"

To make matters worse I tried to pull enough of my foot out from under Jack so as I could grab the bridle around his nose—but the mean SOB grabbed my arm and chomped down hard as hell, refusing to let go with his buck teeth, and grinding my flesh and bones like I was a mouthful of alfalfa or oats or some darn duende dinner delight.

Finally a car drives by and honks and scares Jack—and me too. Then our neighbor Miss Matthews comes out with her brother, Steve, and helps me get up and going. Her peacocks were calling in the orchard and I felt about as mournful as they seemed. But I was finally free from my beast's clutches, free to cuss him to hell and back, and lead him back to his little shed and then hobble up to the house for emergency medical treatment and any tender words I could get from a mother who never wanted me to have a donkey of any kind, let alone a dumb duende-coached one like Jack. The only good thing that came out of the whole affair is that those not so friendly persuasions led to my getting Tony, a blazed-faced, stocking-footed sorrel horse who was twice as smart as Jack was dumb.

I had to suffer my injury first, however, and the pains started pretty much when I limped into the living room and found my mother talking with this dressed up older guy in a suit and tie who, to my ear, talked kind of like a girl. I tagged him right off as a sissy, a nice enough guy but real effeminate, and an indoor man for sure. They were looking out the front window and he was measuring the sill and talking about the drapes and saying, "A heavier fabric would be best, both to retard the dust and block more of the afternoon sun."

My mother interrupted him and came to my aid right away, going to the kitchen, breaking open an ice tray, and bringing me a tea-towel ice pack. I sat down in a big easy chair, celebrating the coolness of the ice, which felt much more soothing than mother's frenzied words, "Gracious, Rory...we're getting rid of that animal once and for all! Mr. Mitchell and I are just finishing up. So rest easy for a bit."

Mr. Mitchell expressed his sincere sympathy and then turned back to flipping through his fabric samples and holding up a rose colored floral drapery swatch, saying, "This is exquisite, Mrs. Strayhope, just perfect for adding energy and exuberant panache to the room!"

"I agree, oh yes I agree, but just leave the sample here and let me live with it for a while, show it to Mr. Strayhope, and I'll get back to you first thing next week. As you can see, my boy here needs an aspirin and some rest."

"Maybe a popsicle would help ease the pain," pipes up Mr. Mitchell as he leaves and heads for his car. Suddenly he seemed like a much nicer man than I first thought.

§

I limped around the house a bit and then went out to feed Jack some alfalfa and see that he had water. Maybe he'd tell me if Satherine had talked to him about tricksters. I knew my father would ask me if I did my chores and I was proud of always taking care of the animals even when I was mad at them or myself. They were dependent on how we took care of them. And we had quite a few different kinds there on our acre of land: horses, a cow, chickens, a dog, three or four cats, and now and then a hog since my dad loved his bacon and eggs and his wilted lettuce salad drizzled with bacon grease. He was a real country boy, and grew up on bacon, biscuits, and gravy on a back woods farm in the Oklahoma hills where livestock wasn't so much a hobby as a means of survival.

My dog, a big tri-colored collie named Skipper, followed me around as usual, and, always barked at the chickens when we passed the chicken coop and Lucinda's memory. He'd start to growl about thirty yards from Jack's shed and I always tried to keep them separated since Skipper would go for Jack's legs and got him good once before he got the Sweet Jesus kicked out of him. All the time I was getting the alfalfa and the water I kept thinking, despite my aches and pains, about how nice this sissy fellow was dressed—gray sharkskin suit with a purple tie and a bountiful handkerchief flowing out of his coat pocket. He even had a small flower in his lapel, maybe a carnation or a periwinkle or some floral enhancement, which was a far cry from the giant gladiola designs in the drapery material he wanted Mother to buy. Stop to think of it, Mr. Mitchell kind of reminded me of Miss Matthews' peacocks.

"Resplendent flowers, a virtual cornucopia of Flora's majesty," he told Mother as if he really knew what he was talking about and believed in his work—something more than a sales spiel. As for me, my pants were still coated with road dust and dried saliva drilled into my arm from old Jack's slobbery mouth hold.

I finished my chores and told Jack it would be a cold day in hell when Satherine and I would forgive him and he might as well start counting his remaining hospitable days. But I didn't mean it and still loved the old raunchy guy. After all, it was Grandma who reminded me, that Jesus himself rode a donkey in to Jerusalem and that a burro was an honored beast of burden for all kinds of people including prospectors in the old West. My "apology" was made all the harder by the pain in my leg and wrist. I mean I could barely make it back to the house and had little or nothing to say to Skipper when he wanted to romp around like usual. My dad was home and asked all about it, saying it would all be better by morning. "Just be glad you don't have polio, Rory, where we'd have to put you in an iron lung!"

That got me thinking back to when they closed Tingley Beach just the same week I'd been swimming there and had even made it out to the floating deck in the middle of the lake. There was a polio scare throughout the city then and I guess the whole Southwest if not the entire United States and maybe the world.

We'd seen an exhibit of iron lungs at the State Fair with manikins inside and movies with real kids in the long, ugly steel cylinders, and listened to recordings explaining how "These marvelous machines will do the breathing for their occupants." They were horrible looking contraptions, all sealed up with just a head sticking out one end and little windows to peak through allowing you only to see the deformed body inside. It was as if Sally Pacheco's withered hand and Dickie's shrunken foot, were more than a hand or a foot, but extended to legs and arms and all kinds of crippling skeleton twists and turns.

If kids made it out of the iron lung they couldn't walk and had to have special crutches and shoes and had to hold out decorated cans and jars for coins and contributions for victims everywhere. The State Fair recording said adults were also susceptible and could be affected too.

In the early evening Satherine applied her special mix of tobacco, nicotine, and crushed mint leaves to my arm, competing with Grandma who insisted on wrapping my calf and ankle with brown paper and string all doused with vinegar. Both women's remedies were cooling but, in spite of all the attention neither one stopped the pain...just smelled funny, especially the nicotine juice which Satherine had soaked up from the bowl of my dad's old Falcon pipe.

Then at bedtime I had a couple of aspirin, some generously applied

Watkins liniment, mixing with the other stuff, a heating pad turned on high, and the usual prayers said in the true hope that, "If I should die before I wake, I pray the Lord my soul to take." Grandma's bedroom was next to mine, and tonight she chose to read aloud what she considered a comforting story about Lucifer and his fall from heaven. She'd come to live with us after my granddad died and she had all kinds of home remedies and folk sayings and could quote the Bible and McGuffey's Reader cover to cover, at times confusing which was which. Somehow she and Satherine competed for the family's good graces, but Satherine went home at night and Grandma didn't.

Satherine lived off of Tapia Road in an old gray-stuccoed house with a tin roof. What I remember most about the yard, the times we'd take her home, was that the dirt around her little yard was swept clean, down to the hard clay surface at her doorstep. What her life was like inside her house I could only wonder, knowing only that odds were it was cleaner than clean, just like Satherine herself.

I guess the story about Lucifer, thoughts about Satherine's mysterious if not supernatural private life, and the conflicting odors of all the medicinal remedies I had on my arm, and leg are what charged up my dreams...but I can assure you there wasn't anything comforting about them.

§

Inside the iron lung was like being in a diving bell. My head was free, sticking out the hole in the east end, toward the mountains. And I wanted to run along the trails and smell the pine and see the iridescent blue-black mountain jays, but they were picking at my leg, merging with the bruises, and then hopping up to my arms and picking at the teeth marks on my arm, thinking they were huge kernels of corn and my arm an elongated corn cob. But I couldn't scare them away! My arms and legs wouldn't move and then suddenly I was outside the iron lung, looking through the small thick-layered glass window and inside was the duded up drapery guy, looking all beautiful like Lucifer at the time of his fall. He was all wrapped up in the floral material he had shown my mother. And then he turned and smiled at me with a donkey face and a mouth full of donkey teeth, and he was moaning and braying and calling for "Mrs. Strayhope, Mrs. Strayhope.... I'm coming over to the house to see you." And then he threw the heavy drape material aside and exposed a steel skeleton, constructed of the large wrought iron curtain rods in our living room, the kind with chiseled arrowheads at the tips—and between his leg was a long curtain rod which on closer look was his penis, much longer than old Jack's long donkey dong, and split into two serpent heads with tongues lashing out both tips! And then he started to throw open the top of the iron lung and started climbing out, his steel bones striking the iron lung and vibrating like the two prongs of a giant tuning fork which had vibrated off the shelf next to a small guitar and he kept strumming the shaft between his legs, hobbling around, now outside the lung, and heading straight for me with a paper donkey tail and a straight pin! But I couldn't really move to avoid him, though somehow Skipper was there and Satherine too and Skipper grabbed the man's leg and held him while Satherine helped me crawl back into the iron lung. Then my father came on the scene and slammed the door closed and ran to tackle the man, but he was impaled on the long arrowhead-tipped curtain rod the Lucifer-like salesman held up to him. Then he swathed father in the drapery material and the flowers and vines began to grow and tightened around him and he lay there gasping for breath. I tried to blow the strong, stinking vapors from my arm and leg to help him breathe, but they could not escape the iron lung and soon had overcome me and carried me into black oblivion.

§

I don't really know when I awakened but it was still dark in my bedroom and I was perspiring and my throat was dry and I coughed and I heard Grandma through the wall, snoring and wheezing, and I lay there in the dark hallucinating, thinking that the devilish drapery salesman was outside my door, knocking and trying to get in, fighting with Jesus who was softly and tenderly calling me home, turning the knob and peering through the diamond shaped window in my outside door. Then a distorted vision of the duende flashed before me, all teeth with flowing white hair and light bulb eyes, and I rolled over onto the floor and tried to walk into the bathroom but I couldn't stand and could barely crawl on the hard, rough–carpeted floor and then just as I was ordering new, plush carpet from Lucifer, it all went dark again.

§

Next morning Father had to carry me to the breakfast table to nibble on some Wheaties, but I had no appetite. I kept thinking about my nightmare and all I really wanted was some salty bean broth. However, Mother said I'd have to wait until Satherine boiled up a kettle of pinto beans—maybe for supper. I drank some cold orange juice and finally got my legs under me and resisted but I had to go with mother to Sun Drug for more aspirin and then to the home decorating store to finalize the drapery selection.

Sun Drug was always appealing since they had all kinds of toiletries—for both men and women. And the aromas were great, exotic shave and skin creams and straight razors, and talc, powders, astringents, and hair dressings and so many colors of lipstick it put the Duncan yoyo inventory to shame. So I could always find fascinating things on the aisles and in the display cases. The pharmacists were always crisp and clean, their smocks starched stiffer than Nita's custom-stitched jeans. This time I was pretty woozy and finally had to sit down at the soda fountain until Mother finished.

"Do you think you can make one more stop? I thought you'd be better by now. I'm beginning to get worried about you. If you're not better soon I'm calling Doc Heywood"

When we got to "Modern Home Décor" store I could barely read the big sign with large letters arcing over a couch like a rainbow. All I could really see was lots of colors, yellows merging with blacks into a green background. I was able to drag my fogged-over brain and rubbery body through the door and plop down in the first big chair I could find. It was like a huge living room with lots of chairs and end tables and divans all crowded together with no determination of function. Carpets and curtains, bedrooms and breakfast tables, it made no difference. One room serving all purposes as far as my groggy eyes could see. I started to doze but was brought up short by Mr. Mitchell feeling my forehead with his clammy, white, big veined hand. I heard some talk about the power of prayer and pushing the liquids, and the next thing I knew I was home in bed taking aspirin and drinking water.

§

I awakened to voices and some four or five people surrounding by bed. I couldn't really tell how many since the blur was back and I was seeing double. I heard them saying things like, "Illness is often psychological. The boy may think he has polio but he really doesn't. He's imagining things. Prayers are the answer. Let us pray together in the name of Jesus Christ and rid this youngster's mind of superstition and false beliefs. Rise and walk, rise and walk...we pray in Jesus' holy name."

I swooned and suddenly I saw Jesus come into the room on a donkey, waving a palm branch. It wasn't just Jesus on any donkey though, I swear. It was Jesus...on old Jack! Then Jesus turned to me, real close like and said, "Bless you my child! Be kind to the poor, be they donkey or man. Think about what it would be like to be a donkey, your Jack. He minds as well as can be expected. Remember that I rode a donkey like Jack."

§

I guess all the praying worked. In a few days I was up and wobbling around the house, walking outside and smelling the lilacs and spirea, and ready again to take old Jack out for a ride. When I put his bridle on him he didn't lay his ears back or anything. He let out a donkey greeting or two but it was kind of tame sounding, not nearly as loud and sustained as usual. I whispered in his ear to take me on a nice ride like he did Jesus and not to listen to duende and lie down in the middle of the road—that I was still sore from our last misadventure.

Then I noticed that his tail was braided! "What the devil?" I uttered as we headed out onto the road. "Damn dreams! Damn duende!" I yelled. I surmised that something, some spirit, had braided not just his tail but also his brain. No one, not Satherine, not Jesus, not his mother Mary, not my mother, and certainly not I could figure out old Jack. I always rode him bare back, just a bridle and had no trouble since he was such a slow poke. This time he acted up as soon as he hit the road and I bounced around on my tailbone so hard I couldn't stay on. I jumped off right in from of Miss. Matthews' house about the same spot where the damn burro stopped last time when I injured my leg and arm. And old Jack? Something even more mysterious than the duende had him. This time he started braying, went into a fast walk, then a trot, and then a gallop and kept on running into the orchard, dodging the trees and peacocks, kicking up his heels, then disappearing into the greenery, never to be found.

I think of him now and then, especially at Christmas time when all those nativity scenes crop up and everyone loves donkeys. I sometimes think I hear him braying. And I rub my arm and pray he's somehow playing with the duende, braying and praying a throaty hello to mischief. And every baby Jesus I pass there in the mangers seems to smile, reminding me to be kind if I'm ever tempted to curse at a jackass.

The Good Samaritan

"Thou shalt love...thy neighbor as thyself."
— Luke 10:27, *The Bible*

Maybe it was Sunday school that got Dirk Dawkins off on the wrong foot. Maybe it was Vacation Bible School. Maybe it was that week at Soda Dam youth camp up in the Jemez Mountains. Or maybe it was just church and all its commandments. Maybe it was the people he associated with, his River Rat friends, including me, or maybe it was just him, his personality, the way he was and the way he was meant to be, born to be wild. Whatever it was Little Dirk got into trouble—bad trouble, and he almost took me with him but for the grace of God, if he or she is a god who sorts out the good, the bad, the unsightly, and the downright ugly.

Dirk surely wasn't what you would call a good boy, not from the very first time I met him at Sunday School, although he was a church goer, was baptized, and his father was a deacon—Brother Derek Dawkins was his name and he was always after Dirk, expecting this and expecting that, scolding and criticizing this, complaining and grousing about that. And ugly? Deacon Dawkins had a horrific voice! Not fit for radio you might say, or even pleasant conversation. His voice was downright scary sounding, if you will. He had some kind of an electric voice box implant and he'd have to touch his throat and somehow activate the little amplifier to talk. It was filled with static, even feedback and to me was just downright babel. Plus he always wrapped his throat in thick gauze to cover what must have been a hole where his larynx should have been— right about where a normal Adam's apple should be. "Like father like son," they say, and you can see why Dirk didn't want to be like his freaky father Derek. Just having similar sounding names was enough to put any father's son on edge.

Well, Little Dirk, everyone called him—not to confuse him with his father—if such a thing were possible since everyone called Little Dirk's father Derek or just "D." It might have confused some since Big D's son was Little D, similar initials and all making for a kind of redundant relationship. It might have been even more confusing for some since father Derek and son Dirk were bad, ugly, and downright aggravating to be around.

How could a church deacon be bad you might ask—that is, if you hadn't been a churchgoer? He was good with a smile and people rather pitied him, not being able to talk normally, but his handicap ugliness was more than all that. Every other word the man said was either "Goddamn" or "Jesus fucking Christ" or some variant expression of breaking the commandment about not taking the Lord's name in vain. Rumor had it that he banged the good Reverend Grant's young wife at least once or maybe twice a month—depending on which churchgoer you were talking to. How anyone could stand hearing "I love you," or other words of endearment from that scratchy porcupine voice is beyond me. He carried around a cassette recording of the Bible, which he could switch on through his throat amplifier. If that wasn't strange, hearing Matthew, Mark, Luke, and John speaking from Deacon Derek's throat, I don't know what is. It could put the fear of God into you if you didn't know the background of just how daily cigar smoking and throat cancer led to such spooky pronouncements.

Every time there would be a baptism Brother Derek would assist, making sure the baptistry was filled to the right level, helping Preacher Grant with his hip boots, extending a hand to lead the dripping and gasping reborn up the slippery, waterlogged stairs. And every time some body was saved and took those timorous steps up to accept the Lord and declare their sinful ways Brother Derek would holler and yell out an amplified barrage of "Halleluiah! Jesus saves! Jesus saves! Yes, brethren, yes! Goddamn right he does!" Praise the Lord!" How he kept from electrocuting himself and the water-soaked others with his static-generating throat radio is beyond me.

I remember him actually pushing Little Dirk up the aisle to commit to Christ, to declare he was once lost but recently found, once blind but could now see while Mrs. Hetzel pumped away, playing "Just as I Am" on the wheezing church organ. "Just as Derek wanted his son Dirk to be" should really have been the words. Connie Grant, the good reverend's wife dabbed her eyes and scrunched her face, and squawked out loud just like it must have sounded when the Deacon D put it to her behind the baptistry.

§

Shortly after he was saved, Little Dirk Dawkins pulled a knife on me. We were learning about the Good Samaritan and how he stopped to help this poor soul along the side of the road over there in the holy land somewhere between Jerusalem and Jericho or some sandy place, when I feel this hard, sharp-pointed gouge in my side just like Christ on the cross, and amidst my pain-laden "Ouch!" I hear Littler Dirk giggling and saying, "Shut your fucking mouth fart-face or I'll push it into your Jesus-loving side!" And I look down and see Dirk's holding a pocketknife against my ribs—the kind of fat, multi-blade, screwdriver, can opener, finger nailfile knife that darn near makes your pocket look like you've got one hell of a hard on, what with the bulge and all! Who knows how he carried it "concealed," since it looked twice as big as Little Dirk's dick.

"You say something, son?" Mr. Terrill, our Sunday school teacher, asked Dirk. Then I heard the blade click closed and Dirk's sugarcoated, cough-syrupy voice say, "Nope, just thinking about how they stabbed the Lord in his side there on the cross and how everyone should be a good neighbor like Sam the Samaritan!"

"Yes, Dirk, Jesus suffered terribly for our sins but he is our Good Samaritan and looks down on us daily to save and protect us."

"Say, Mr. Terrill, sir," Dirk asked, "when are we gonna study Lucifer and how the prettiest and best angel in heaven, the brightest star up there, was cast down to earth by God, and how he still made the best of his situation?"

All the while I wanted protection! That's what I needed when it came from Little Dirk Dickhead's bullying. "Prick face little devil!" I said to him as he secretly folded back the blade and smiled his baleful smile. I tried not to sit anywhere near the mean little bastard after that.

Then at Vacation Bible School, I was appointed to carry the church flag and I was just raising it up when Dirk grabbed it away from me and started spearing the kids lined up behind us, taunting them by repeating, "Onward, onward all you chicken–shit Christian soldiers!" Mrs. Beckman tried to ignore the commotion and started her Roberta Sherwood drumming on her cooking pan, trying to get the right march tempo for us all to sing our way into the sanctuary, which for us was shelter from Dirk's definition of being an honor guard—what with his swashbuckling swipes and swoops, pokes and jabs.

§

When it came time for all the church kids to head up to the Soda Dam Youth Camp for a week in July, I tried to beg off, telling my folks that I didn't want to leave my dog, Skipper, who was getting a little old and depended on me for food and water and petting and overall kindness. In truth I depended much more on Skip's companionship than he depended on me—but it was mutual love whatever the equation. I knew he was as brave as the dog in the song, "Old Shep," and would have saved me from any danger, including Little Dirk Dawkins had I the chance to sick him on the pygmy devil.

"Oh, don't you mind Skip," came the parental chorus. "We'll take good care of him and bring him up to see you for a romp in the mountains at the end of the week."

So it was off to camp and, you guessed it, my destined bunkmate was one Dirk Dawkins and I felt certain that I would probably never see my dog or my parents again. For darn sure I'd never get to poke the good Reverend Grant's wife, daughter, sister, cousin or anyone else for that matter if he had his way with that Medici multi-blade menace of his.

The camp was pretty enough, nestled away in the picturesque Jemez Mountains, just a couple of hours north of the city. The dam was a natural phenomenon created over the years by increasing layers of mineral rock and a river ran through it to form nearby pools of mineral water where one could baptize or soak away their soiled soul, sore muscles, and aching joints. There were fish in the river, lots of Rainbow trout, which were stocked annually. And just a mile or so from the dam was this big outcrop of granite rock all shaped like a ship. Its name was "Battleship Rock." It was no "Rainbow Mountain," that's for sure.

There were activities: baths planned at the springs, fishing in the East Fork of the Jemez River, and hikes up Battleship Rock. Nights were for roasting wieners and marshmallows, listening to story telling, singing hymns, or, like the church bulletins advertised, having a rollicking hootenanny, or listening to a string quartet play Dvorak under a myriad of stars, deciphering the wind whispers in the towering trees, and inhaling their pine needle perfume—all leading, ideally, to blissful sleep, had it not been for Little Dirk and his troubled ways.

The ride up in the bus wasn't too bad—just some glowering stares and a fuck you finger now and then. Most of Dirk's animosity there was spent on Wilson Hoffiens, a frail little kid who would have been afraid of his own shadow had he enough meat on his bones to cast a shadow. "Hey skinny," Dirk would taunt him, "Better roll up the window or you'll blow away!" Or he'd lean over and say to Wilson, "Can't you keep your Goddamn bones from rattling every time we hit a bump?" "Hey bub, do you got any balls?" It was just one taunt after another, poking fun at the skeleton kid. And there wasn't any use to ask him to let up because that just stoked his ire. No body had the courage to make fun of Dirk and how short he was. He was like a damn terrier dog that would bite your ankle with needle-shape teeth and hold on until you kicked it off.

§

When we got to our cabin Dirk ordered everyone where to sleep, saying he was the dorm domo and needed the lower bunk closest to the door so he could do guard duty. Mr. Terrill was our sponsor and Dirk could do no wrong, never allowing the trusting, good-hearted old shit to doubt the ways of good Christian fellowship. His cabin was a good hundred or two hundred yards away so once lights were out we were on our own and Dirk was out the door running naked around our cabin, pissing on every rock and bush and telling Hoffiens and me and some others to do the same or else, and making fun of everyone's anatomy, of course. It was kind of fun for a time until a tree branch would slap you in the face or you tripped over a boulder. That was seen as just the horseplay of first night initiation.

His campaign platform was simple: "Unless you want to keep finding hellgrammites in your food...when we have elections, remember you've chosen me to be in charge." It wasn't worth denying that.

§

Next day we all hiked over to the dam and climbed around through its little caverns made by the stream and over the rounded dome which was both slippery and high, about fifty feet over the rushing waters. Dirk called anyone a chicken that didn't follow, being the self-appointed captain of all us "chicken-shit Christian" soldiers as he called us. Hoffiens was bringing up the rear, scared to death you could tell. And in one of the caverns Dirk sneaks behind and around Hoffiens and gives him an elbow nudge and down he slides—and would have hit the rushing water had he not caught hold of a sulfur stalagmite at the last minute. We all heard him whimpering for help and turned around to see Dawkins leaning down with that same diabolical Sunday school, sulfur-smelling smile on his face to offer the poor skinny kid an unsteady hand.

Wilson didn't want to complain to Terrill, bone scared, as it were, and the rest of us just accepted it as a close call. But given what happened a couple of days later when we hiked up Battleship Rock, we should have said something, should have given poor Wilson our congregational Christian soldier protection.

You must realize that it's impossible to scale the face of that rock. The only way to the top, unless you're a professional mountain climber, is to approach it from the back, making lots of trail turns and circling back on yourself with one hairpin turn after another. Luckily, I remembered how I was taught to climb a hill pretty much sideways, at a diagonal, on the sides of your shoes, rather than digging in your toes and taking frontal steps like climbing a ladder. We had to cross several little canyons and a couple of big ones to make it almost to the top, to what would be the bow of the battleship. We all made the crossings and the necessary leaps, lending a hand where needed. A couple of us had to pull Wilson along but we coaxed him to persevere. "But fellows," he'd softly lament, "I'm afraid of heights."

When we got to the top edge and looked down you could see how really high we were. Wilson didn't want to approach the edge and hung back—until Dirk got right in his face and called him a mamma's nipple boy and dared him to walk right to the edge. He shouldn't have taken the dare. We shouldn't have let Dirk tease him into doing it—because when he did inch, step by hesitant step, to the edge, Dirk yelled out "Shitty sissy-pants sissy!" as loud as he could and poor Wilson was over the edge, tumbling head first, slamming into the jagged rocks below, sounding like a gunny sack of dried pinto beans, thud to thud to thud, accompanied by little whimpering, rattling baby cries.

"Bombs away!" was all Dirk said, against our screams, and turned away heading back down the trail in a carefree lope.

§

"Tragic accident at church camp: boy slips and falls down the face of Battleship Rock." That's how Mr. Terrill and the local paper described it, never mentioning Dirk Dawkins' name in any public account, especially at church. But the disturbed kid would see plenty made of his name in the papers when he joined the army—and then some years later after we'd all tried to forget Little Dirk Dawkins and his deacon dad, even the ghost of the skinny kid we Christian soldiers chickened out on named Wilson Hoffiens.

Dirk came back once on furlough from the army special forces and told us all how he'd learned to kill with anything at hand, a boot lace, a can opener, a tin-can lid, and especially his serrated combat knife. Then we didn't hear from him again and only put it all together when we read the news account.

It seems he had settled in Texas after his discharge and married an ill-fated woman with a couple of kids. Reverend Grant, his aroused, spunky, nympho spouse, Mrs. Hetzel, Deacon Derek Dawkins and most of the old timers I knew, including Mr. Terrill, had long since passed on and I was now the music director at a cross town church, always making it a point to include at least one of the old hymns remembered from the Sunday services of my youth.

It was Mr. Terrill's widow one revival Sunday who handed me the news clipping, while my own wife and kids waited for me in a hot car with the sun blazing down and Evelyn, my wife, sitting there fanning herself with the church bulletin.

"Did you hear about the Dawkins boy? And he was such a good Christian. I guess the war made him do it." That's when those long ago Sunday school lessons about the Good Samaritan came back to me as I started to read:

FORMER CITY RESIDENT EXECUTED

"Derek (Dirk) Dawkins, age thirty-one, was executed in the Texas state prison in Huntsville on May 3, 1971 for the murder of his wife and his two step-children, ages 8 and 10. Dawkins, who resided in Stephenville, Texas where he had settled after serving three years in the U.S. Army, grew up here. His father, Derek Dawkins, Sr., who was a deacon in and a founding member of the Valley Baptist Church, preceded him in death. Young Dawkins had been dishonorably discharged after shooting and paralyzing a fellow infantryman in a dispute over a bottle of hot sauce in a popular Bar-B-Q eatery. Anger and domestic bad blood seemed to continue to plague him after his marriage, friends saying that he was frequently in public arguments with his wife and neighbors. An emergency call for help from his wife resulted in police arriving at the home only to find Dawkins sitting at the kitchen table reading the Bible, his wife and children all stabbed to death. Investigators said, in an ironic coda, that the Bible was opened to the story of the Good Samaritan. And that the knife bookmarked the passage, "Go and do likewise.""

When the clipping dropped from my hand, and shimmered away in the Sunday noonday breeze, I wasn't so much stunned at such a story of suffering and shame, as I was guilt-ridden—remorseful that somehow, some way, even after he forced Wilson Hoffiens off Battleship Rock, I hadn't tried to help the crazy son of a bitch that day in Sunday School when he pulled a knife on me while we were learning how to be a Good Samaritan. Leaving me asking "Where the hell's help when you really need it?"

Smitten

"The bird is done when the breast meat reads 170 degrees F and that of the thigh meat is at 185 degrees F."
—*Fanny Farmer Cookbook*

R.J. Strayhope was prone to speed and disregard road conditions and traffic signs—all for the feel of the car, the sound of the motor, the fresh evening air hitting his face through the rolled down windows. There was plenty of power at his feet, three linked deuce carburetors, and a big 348 V-8 Chevy motor. He was devoted to keeping the Impala tuned and polished—always a purr, ever a shine.

This evening he was thinking about her as usual and where he was headed...up-town, to the Heights. The route would take him by the airport and the military jets, which thrilled him so much with their noise and powerful flight. He would sit with her in the car on the western edge of the runway late into the night, watching the airliners come in, and once in a while a fighter plane, maybe a Thunderbird flying in from California or an Air National Guard F-100 Super Saber jet.

Crossing the river was sweet with the aroma of Russian Olive trees and their precious little yellow flowers made all the more pungent by the river water churning the sand bars and banks, mixing everything muddy brown with its frothy foam, enhancing the growing fragrances of night wafting through the open windows. The nighthawks swooped and dived, their radar pinging with each insect hit like the armament from a fighter plane. He twisted and turned the steering wheel in imitation of their flight. Jet or bird, tonight he was in a hurry.

She had her own special perfume, sweeter than the olive blossoms, sweeter than honeysuckle, and soon he would be able to breathe it into his nostrils, inhaled down into his lungs, breaths made all the sweeter by the bevy of kisses that awaited him. Only vaguely did he see the engorged fire hose stretched across the street as he came down the Coal Avenue overpass. He felt the tires bump and the bounce of the shock absorbers, and the scrape of the coil springs, heated and weakened in the worship of looking low-rider cool. The rattle of the visor over his head grew louder, merging with voices of the men in helmets pointing the big nozzle at the corner grocery store on Broadway he'd passed a hundred times. Out of the corner of his eye he saw that the firemen were waving and yelling at him to slow down.

Then out of the smoky air a motorcycle cop pulled him over and the ticket was for $85.00—way too much money, much more than his last tickets for speeding and running a red light. The fines seemed to be mounting. And with this one went a court date. "No way will I miss this court appearance, gringo fallado. See you in court," the cop said with a smirk. "Yeah, see you there, sir," the kid said in a whisper, subduing and trailing off the words "uppity beaner."

He was running late but made up the time and when he got to Margot's house she was just beginning to worry. "The movie starts in fifteen minutes, Rory. We're gonna miss the previews and short subjects."

The Cactus Drive-in was only a few miles away and by the time he paid the dollar admission, wheeled into the chosen slot, took the speaker off the hook, and placed it on his window a preview for a Charlton Heston movie called "Ben-Hur" was just ending.

"See, Sugar, we made it. By the time I get back with the Cokes the feature will just be starting." "Better hurry," she said.

He could see Howard Keel and Russ Tamblyn moving around on the screen and by the time he opened the door to hand over the refreshments, the music came on and the story of "Seven Brides for Seven Brothers" had started. He'd wanted to see "The Americano" with Glenn Ford at the Terrace but Margot wanted to see this movie. "Musicals are so much fun, Rory. You'll like it I know. And the snuggles and kisses made up for what he didn't pay any attention to, thinking when he came up for air about the ticket and the cop and the future court date.

After the movie they parked outside Margot's house for a time, until the porch light started blinking on and off—the usual signal that it was time for her to go in. And he was off, waiting to rev the motor and squeal the tires when he pulled out onto Gibson—then the trek west back across the river. There were hardly any cars on the road and the grocery store had been saved from total incineration, so he made good time home, again, thinking about the sweetness of the night and Margot—and the drag of facing another ticket.

"This time they'll probably throw the book at me and take my license away." And his last prayerful words when he hit the sheets in the back bedroom were, "Damn it to hell. All for running over a shitty fire hose!"

Thanksgiving wasn't far off, just a day or two after his court date, and the invitation to have dinner with Margot and her family was impossible to turn down. "They don't have to know," he fooled himself into believing, knowing too that her father was the District Attorney and a hard-boiled law and order type who was always talking about civic duty and the blessings of citizenship in this great country of ours. R.J. had heard more than one sermon on that. He disliked judgments of all kinds. Yes, he'd keep it a secret. Not even tell Margot. Face the judge who would know Rory's father and, miracle of all miracles, dismiss the case. After all, Bobby Jess Strayhope was a prominent Valley businessman and had even run for County Commissioner. His "Vote for Me Too" slogan hadn't quite done the trick and Benny "Cerveza" Alvarez got in promising free drinks at the Buckhorn for every delivered vote. Bobby Jess knew people—but mostly in the county. This ticket was a city offense.

§

Rory showed up at the downtown courthouse on time and, after the security check, sat quietly in the back of the room. When the bailiff called him he was escorted to a side room and to his surprise there was Margot's father, Marvin Metcalf, LLD, standing next to the judge who was just putting on his imposing black robe.

"Rory R.J. Strayhope is it? Charged with fire hose violation—interfering with public safety, eh? And you're the boyfriend of the good D.A.'s daughter. Is that the picture? What do you think we should do with you? Can't have a black spot on the name of a civic official, now can we, especially not on the eve of a statewide campaign? Should we throw him in the hoosegow, Marvin? Your verdict?"

"Hell, Geoffrey, it's a crime any would-be Romeo would make on the way to see his Juliet. Just sorry to say it's my Juliet and she's smitten with this teen-age troubadour. What if you dismiss the case and erase all record from the police log? The officer's not going to show anyway, according to my sources."

"Well then, it's your lucky day, son. Thanks to an understanding D.A. and a caring father who monitors his daughter's associates. I've got a full docket today anyway. So go back out and when the clerk calls your name and the absent officer's, I'll say 'case dismissed,' and you leave a free man. But it's the last favor you'll get from me, Strayhope, thanks to this man, so clean up your act."

"My advice," Metcalf said, "just between us, is cool it with Margot. Just fade away after this Thanksgiving dinner invitation I hear about. We'll keep this little conference confidential. Good behavior through Thanksgiving and then...and then you drop Margot or I'll see to it that she drops you. Just find another girlfriend, a dumb one preferably. We want a reputable Republican boyfriend during my upcoming gubernatorial bid—not the river rat likes of you. I'm due back to the office. And thanks Geoff. I owe you one of Rachel's extra dirty martinis at the Elks' Club."

"Sure thing, Marv, remember me when you get to the Round House. And, say, how's Elizabeth these days? Staying with the program?"

"About a year now since Turquoise Lodge. Keeping my fingers crossed she doesn't fall off the wagon before the election."

§

Thanksgiving came faster than Rory hoped, afraid of just how his hushed up meeting with the judge and Margot's father would play a week or two later. He knew the old man wanted to keep his good name from being besmirched by, in his eyes, a teenage motor head he wished his daughter would forget. But there would be holiday family there to buffer what the good D.A. alluded to as "strained relations," that day in the judge's chambers.

Rory, by design, pulled up slowly in front of Margot's house at exactly 4:30 pm, and turned off the grumbling motor. It was a cold day with snow in the mountains and a dusting on the west mesa around the volcanoes. He'd gotten up before sunrise to drive down to Tomé Hill with his brother in law, Herbert, for an early pheasant hunt. They'd bagged two roosters and, by mistake, a hen. Then back home to dress the birds for his family's dinner. A shower and a quick meal to please his relatives—everyone careful to watch for the residual little lead bb's potentially hiding in each bite of bird. He said he had to rush, and arranged—over parental protests and groans—to have his favorite apple pie and ice cream saved until he got back from dinner with his girlfriend.

"Apple pie without cheese is like a kiss without a squeeze, R.J.!"

Brother Herbert had piped up, "So get that kiss and that squeeze regardless." That would be the real dessert, and he imagined the lovely face of Margot when she greeted him.

Margot's house wasn't a large or even a well-furnished house. Just an average flat-roof, imitation pueblo tract construction with a front and back lawn and some landscaping which Marvin seemed to take pride in maintaining, always pruning or watering in his undershirt and old khakis every time Rory visited.

Today everyone was dressed up, Margot in a tailored gray flannel skirt and a ruffled white blouse and black flats. It was a becoming outfit and she looked radiant. "You know my brother Eddie, and this is his friend Pablo from school. Dad and mom are in the kitchen with the turkey." And Margot hollered around the corner, "Mom, Dad, Rory's here now—and I know he's hungry waiting this late for dinner."

"Take his coat to the bedroom, dear, Mrs. Metcalf replied, sounding a bit nervous with a quiver in her voice. The turkey's...almost ready, just a bit more basting and we'll eat."

There was some deep voiced grumbling but no real hello from the man of the house who was too busy scolding his wife in a gruff reprimand, "Liz, are you damn sure you're steady and the turkey is done?"

§

Margot ushered Rory into her parent's bedroom just off the short hallway, and with one hand he tossed his coat on the bed while looking up for the day's first clandestine kiss and reached out for the caress he'd waited for since morning. He was uncomfortable in such intimate surroundings, however, and he couldn't help notice a holstered revolver on the dresser, made all the more menacing and out of place because of its mirror image, showing what appeared to be a snub nosed .38 nickel-plated Smith & Wesson in a fancy, hand-tooled shoulder holster—the elastic belt wrapped around the trigger guard and hammer.

"What's with the gun, Margot?" Rory asked.

"Oh, that's Dad's. It's for protection at work. He's going to run for governor too, and that can be dangerous I guess. It's part of his security. He even has body guards from APD and the state police."

Rory went over to the dresser to take a closer look at the pistol and confirm what caliber it was. As he reached for the silver, turquoise studded grips, Margot said in a loud commanding voice, "Better not touch it! Nobody can. Strict orders."

§

After some small talk about the pros and cons of fraternities and sororities—Eddie was in favor of joining one, Pablo saying he'd die a GDI—they all seated themselves at the dining room table, each place designated by Mr. Metcalf. His wife, looking flushed from the heat of the kitchen, and flustered by figuring out the time and sequence of preparing the turkey just right, brought in the bird in a quaint, floral platter, which she said, was her mother's. "I've followed all of Fanny Farmer's recipes for Thanksgiving dinner." And she listed the sweet potatoes, the green beans, the lime Jell-O with shredded carrots, the creamed corn, the sage dressing, the garlic mashed potatoes and giblet gravy. She was clearly proud but Rory couldn't tell whether she was just flushed from all the work or somehow tipsy or embarrassed and worried that somehow she hadn't pleased her husband and the family.

Everyone except the D.A. at the head of the table assured her that everything was beautiful and delicious looking. Eddie chimed up, "Gee Mom, it's great! I can't wait to dig in." His father cleared his throat to announce that a Thanksgiving blessing was the first order of business and instructed everyone, "Time to bow your heads." Margot winked at Rory and nudged his leg under the table. Eddie batted his eyes as if to tell Pablo, "You've got to indulge the old guy."

When the words came they sounded more like a practice run for a campaign speech than a prayer of gratitude. He emphasized the importance of a land of the free and the home of the brave, the need for a country of laws and stressed, "We must have good police, good prosecutors, and tough judges who, beyond compromise and corruption, will see that the laws are enforced to the letter." "We are blessed," he continued, "in this fine, free land of ours, with elections and the right for each man to vote his conscience, and ward off hooliganism."

Rory peeked over the steaming turkey and the carefully prepared meal to see Mrs. Metcalf dab at her eyes and nose with a napkin, feeling despite Margot's footsy games, that a word or two of thanks about the food and the cook, like his own father had done just hours earlier, would be more in order.

"What a prick!" Rory thought as he crossed himself and finally heard the hypocritical windbag say the final amen.

"Amen, Amen...Amen...Amen...Amen," came the thankful acknowledgments of everyone except Elizabeth Metcalf, who, scooting her chair back, announced, "Oh, I forgot the carving set."

"I hope that's all you forgot, woman!" her husband said. Rory took a long sip of water and wiped away not just the water on his lip but the perspiration beginning to bead on his forehead.

When Mrs. Metcalf handed the long silver-plated, stag-handle knife and wide-tined fork to her husband she said, "I hope everyone enjoys the meal."

Then, then, with the first cut came the outburst: "What the hell, Liz, have you been at the bottle again? This damn turkey isn't done! Look at the blood oozing out of the breast. Can't you fix anything beyond a bologna sandwich? Do I have to call the delicatessen now and have an edible meal delivered? What the shit is wrong with you?"

"Ah, Dad, Eddie said. Mom tried hard working on this. So what if there's a little blood?"

Then the slap across Eddie's face as the long arm of the law reached out and hit his son so hard that the olives he had sneaked for an appetizer flew out of this mouth and across the table.

Margot jumped up and ran to her mother, trying to console her with empty words. Eddie began sobbing, wiping at the blood streaming from his nose, mumbling "Gee, Dad, Geeze!" Pablo got up and left the room, heading back to the safety of the living room. Rory didn't know just what to do other than sit there in stunned silence, trying to comprehend whether he had really witnessed what had just happened.

Before he knew it Mrs. Metcalf ran to the bedroom, her face flooded with tears, and locked the door, saying, "I can't take this anymore. You bastard! You bastard!"

Thus the husband's words: "Drink yourself to death, for all I care.

Find your damn hidden bedroom bottles and guzzle them down into hell."

No sooner than that curse left his lips when a gunshot came from the bedroom, and Rory pictured the Smith & Wesson on the blood-covered bed, and Mrs. Metcalf crumpled on it, her legs akimbo like the drumsticks on the damnable turkey on the table in front of him."

"Oh, Mom, oh Mom!" came Margot's hysterical cry. "See what you've done! See what she's done! See what we've done!" Eddie was back in a flash and Rory was up and together they knocked down the bedroom door. Mrs. Metcalf was seated on the end of the bed with the revolver still in her hand looking at the shattered dresser mirror. "You won't let me go. You won't let me go! I can't stand to look at myself anymore, not anymore! And I can't stand looking at your fat face!"

"I'll call the ambulance and get you back to Turquoise Lodge, dearest. You just won't be able to handle the pressures of my campaign," the frightened, suddenly officious D.A. said, looking around the doorframe to see if he saw a gun, and saying in shaky words, "She has outbursts like this from time to time when she's back on the booze."

"D.A., huh," Rory thought, "You mean "Dumb Ass" he whispered under his breath as he reached out his arms to give Margot a consoling hug. "No chance for him to be governor," she sobbed. "Maybe in hell."

Pachuco

"Quiere combate, gringo?"

As far as I could tell there were only two people in the restroom when I entered. One of them was Chickie Chavez and the other one was Manuel (Manny) Saavedra. They were always together, wherever you saw one you saw the other one: two compadres who stuck together. Chickie was the muscular, tall one, and Manuel, well, he was lithe and medium height, about my size. In grade school, Chickie had thin legs and got the name Chickie. Now Chickie's muscles were bulky and defined, especially his arms, biceps, triceps...but his whole upper chest, pectorals, shoulders, were large. He was no weakling, no stranger to lifting weights, throwing the shot put, and playing center on the football team: The Pile Drivers! He was a pile driver all right and was always bragging about how he had poked Martha Goss so deep she couldn't talk and could barely walk back to class from the ditch.

Manuel wasn't very verbal, and mostly nodded when he was with Chickie, but it was a mistake to think he was dumb. Truth be told, Chickie needed Manny more than Manny needed Chickie...in more ways than one. The longer you were around them you were convinced that, ironically, their respective names somehow fit: Manuel the man, and Chickie the chicken.

Manny was a good-looking hombre and had a way with all the girls, though he never really gave Martha Goss a second look. He had his eye on a couple of the Anglo girls, namely Sandra and Patsy, and regrettably, Linda Louise, who left just about everyone breathless, what with her blonde hair, sparkling gray eyes, full mouth, and creamy complexion. Peaches and cream—that was Linda Lou.

Manny was quick, especially in math and impressed even Mrs. Lefferdink. And a compliment from her, what with her curvaceous body and well rounded ass (no chest to speak of but so what, since from the waist down she was heaven to behold), standing there at the blackboard with chalk in hand guiding us through what was supposed to be algebra. However, we filled in the x's and y's in ways she could never have guessed.

Martha Goss was in the same math class as Chickie, Manny, me, and Thomas Newberry, Rosendo, Ross, and Benny Turrieta—but he insisted on us calling him Benito. Walter Bearfoot was in that class too, and no one could play a better game of basketball or run a better 440 relay than sinewy Bearfoot—unless it was Manny, though he wasn't much for sports letters, although he had a couple.

Much of my trouble with Chickie and Manny, Los Dos Frijoles, as most of my gringo friends called them, started on the ditches—the far drainage ditch which ran behind the school and across the boundary of the Sunset Drive-in theater, and the irrigation ditch which separated the football and baseball fields and the all-weather concrete basketball courts.

This day, Chickie was in front of the restroom mirror, combing his ducktail, and Manny was just turning from the latrine, zipping up his khakis and adjusting the sleeve rolls to their proper position on his Clorox-white T-shirt.

"Well, if it isn't Los Dos Frijoles hanging it out together again. Haven't seen you hombres since you chased me home, 'throwing me with a rock,' as you described it. And before Chicke could put his comb away and finish saying "Chingada tu madre, lambe," smack in the middle of him wadding up his paper towel to toss it into the trash, but before Manny could lift his hand to throw a protective blow, I walked up to Chickie and let him have it full force in the face, hitting his mouth and causing his teeth to cut my knuckles so that you couldn't tell whether the blood was his or mine.

The faucet was still running in the sink and you could hear the last hissing flush of the latrine as I turned and high tailed it out of there, losing myself in the helter-skelter rush of students heading back to class after lunch.

Weeks earlier when I'd run home, tears still visible in my red eyes, after being hit by a barrage of clods on the ditch, my brother-in-law took me aside and gave me some advice: "The best way to beat a bully is to bully him back! The next time you see that greaser pachuco, walk up and hit him in the face, and if he gets his gang after you I'll straighten them out. All the South Valley stompers and Bosque Farms shit kickers will help. You can bet on that."

The gangs then weren't totally defined along ethnic and racial lines, but pachucos were mostly Hispanic, Spanish American or Mexican American. And stompers were Anglos, urban or rural it really didn't matter, but while the pachucos wore white T-shirts and pegged khakis, with snazzy black brogues and thin stylish belts, the stompers wore cowboy boots, western snap-button shirts, Wranglers or Levis and thick belts with big weapon-ready, rodeo-style buckles.

The evolution from just plain kids to either stompers or pachucos started early enough but really took shape in the move from elementary school to middle school and was cemented in high school. The increase in serious violence escalated with each passing grade. Unless drugs got involved, usually marijuana but also cocaine and sometimes heroin, athletics were a kind of neutral ground where jocks didn't really have so much gang loyalty as they did school and team loyalty. Another more or less neutral realm was that of squares, and sissies, four-eyes, and bookworms. But as with all such social stratification there were plenty of exceptions, crossovers, and hybrids.

Eddie Quintana, soon to be known as "Cinco Q" because he came from the Cinco Puntos neighborhood, was my best friend, a neighbor during my younger grade school days. We stuck up for each other regardless—whether with parents, teachers, schoolmates, you name it. We were always there for each other. I had more material things and better clothes, nothing fancy, but not hand me downs like Eddie's, and we could both throw a softball swift as a rocket from centerfield to home plate. And in setback, we could dropkick a football further than it seemed possible to most beholders. We'd help each other and other people too. When Sammy C stepped on a board with a rusty nail in it and drove it all the way through the arch of his foot, we both carried him to the nurse's office and called the school athletic coach, Mr. Rafa Sandoval, (Sandyballs to us). When Joey Casius was so stoned that he crouched up too close to a batter at home plate and got thwacked in the head from a full swing by this big bruiser of a guy named Freddie Frantzen, and lay there twitching in the sand like an epileptic, it was Eddie who picked him up, directing me to clear the way and open the door into old man Hall's pharmacy. And when I accidentally threw a baseball through the window of the principal's office it was Eddie who tried to say he'd done it. Always trying to protect and help. Even as a patrol boy, he was the captain, I was his lieutenant.

But then, just about the time when the move was in store to one of the toughest schools in the city, Eddie moved away—all the way to Los Angeles where his dad got a better job. We didn't even get to say goodbye. One day he was gone and it was Sammy C who told me that our compadre Eddie had left.

So I had to make my way alone, treading lightly between the Stompers and the Pachucos, and the perils of the ditches. Everyone, regardless of classification or affiliation, had to go see Martha Goss at the ditch. If you didn't you were alienated from everybody who was or claimed to be anybody. So I went. I shouldn't have, but I went. Larry Brindleton was the instigator. He was in deep with the stompers. Lots of people were intending to go since it was a Friday afternoon and Martha held forth on Fridays. "She'll turn your balls red, Rory, and there on the ditch bank when you pull your pants down you can actually watch them turn color."

Martha's performance, whatever it turned out to be, was always the hot topic the next Monday. Most of the accounts and descriptions were just plain hard to believe. But curiosity finally got the best of me so I convinced Tommy Newberry, who said he'd been once before, to come with me. Of course, we let Larry lead the way.

Larry was pale complexioned with light brown hair, had a strong, well proportioned body, but globbed pomade on the shock of hair which hung down over his forehead—all of which made him look like a young Hitler or a member of the Nazi youth party you'd see in March of Times newsreels. He wasn't anywhere close to being in the Aryan honor society, not in terms of brains or grades or in terms of aspirations of "honor." He wore fancy hand-carved boots from Mejico with the heels run over and scuffmarks all along the toes. Story was he was kicked out of the Future Farmers of America, though he still wore the organization's faded blue corduroy jacket with yellow embroidered lettering. He was rude and crude and always a clown—far from being a Puritan, or even a Baptist, unless he was a backslider. His older brother, Russell, was a cool guy, two or three years older and a hard worker, a brick layer for a big construction company with lots of contracts up and down the valley, and when you'd see Russell at baseball games he'd sit with his brother, usually with his arm around him, trying to convince Larry not to make untoward bodily noises. He was a master at placing one hand under his armpit and clamping down fast and hard to make a flatulent sound, followed by snorts of yellow-toothed laughter.

So, when seventh period ended that Friday, Larry, Tommy, and I headed off to the ditch to see what we could see—and maybe learn what we could learn beyond the grainy black and white sex education movie we watched in P.E. with running commentary by good old Sandyballs. I just wanted to see if any of the stories going around could possibly be true.

Most of the Monday reports varied from being able to watch Martha do cartwheels, summersaults, and various naked acrobatics to allegedly giving a hand job to Moose Morrissey, the biggest guy around, coming or going, as it were, and mocking Faustino Benevidez by mimicking his wild, profane antics. He was a lanky Mejicano who played first base like Plastic Man and would go around sniffing guys' crotches, grabbing at your privates in the restrooms, then holding his nose and yelling "calzoncillos del soldado! calzoncillos del soldado!" As a result, "Faustino, Faustino, he's our man...if anyone can get your balls, Faustino can," became a chant at basketball games, although a snobby group would say, "Get the ball Faustine."

Martha, everyone said, was non-discriminating and an equal opportunity entertainer who could jump higher and spin longer than any duly elected cheerleader, though she never ran for cheerleader, not in the usual sense, never meeting the grade point or being able to remember the cheers. She was in my Spanish class and was great at Spanglish when she would deign to speak up. Señor Marquez, a suave dresser with a pencil thin Gilbert Roland mustache taught us as much about Spanish music, corridos and rancheros, boleros and all, as he did about Spanish grammar and vocabulary.

Anyway, that Friday we crossed the baseball field and headed for the many cheering voices, as big a roar as you'd ever hear at a Duke's ball game when a hometown player hit a home run. At the ditch there were as many pachucos as there were stompers and everyone was laughing and yelling and cussing and asking Martha to "Do it some more! More! Do it some more, Martha! More Martha, more!"

What she was doing I couldn't see at first, until I pushed around a couple of guys and craned my head so I could see her standing in the drainage ditch in just her underwear. She had long strings of what looked like hair hanging down around her ears and forehead and sticking out of her undergarments. She'd tuck the stuff back into her panties and then pull it out and draw it back and forth between her legs, swaying to and fro...and more than anything suddenly it reminded me of a freak show I'd wandered into and puzzled about at the State Fair a couple of years back or some monster movie at the Sunset Drive-in just a few hundred yards from the cheering crowd. Martha wasn't entertaining at all, just degrading. Not funny...just sad. "What would Mr. Márquez say? Or Herbert, my brother in law?" I surprisingly asked myself.

Turned out that on closer observation it wasn't Martha's hair at all...it was ditch moss and she was picking it up and arranging it on her head, throwing it over her shoulders and even sucking on it like some mermaid Popeye eating putrid strings of canned spinach. The sand of the ditch bottom was churning, turning the clear water murky and, repulsed by it all before I could think I yelled out, "Stop! No More! Basta! Basta! Truchas! Sandy Balls is coming."

Well, the cheering came to a halt and soon all I could hear was my voice, trailing off chanting my spontaneous lie of a warning—my words hanging in the air like the skeins of ditch moss covering poor Martha.

"Suddenly an armada of clods and rocks and all kinds of ditch debris came my direction. Larry himself joined the attack with chants of "Fuck off, man!" and then pachucos and stompers alike, led by Chickie and Manny and Morrissey, united in a kind of claptrap brigade, were chasing me—with Tommy Newberry running, stride by stride, right along side me. Lots of the cowboys and farm kids were laughing, throwing fingers, and waving goodbyes. Faustino was holding his nose and pumping his hips. Talk about a man without a country! Even Martha was madly throwing moss at me, spastically jabbing it with the middle fingers of both hands and kicking sprays of ditch water into the air.

That's what had led me to confide in my brother in law about it and ask his help to redeem myself in the light of such traumatic persecution.

That's what gave me the courage to barge into the restroom and slug Chickie in the mouth.

Waiting for retaliation at any time, some weeks later, and after the Monday morning jabbering and disapproval about what I'd yelled at Martha at the ditch, I was surprised that it came from Celso Davidson one day out on the basketball court. I was sure it would have come from Chickie and Manny, Faustino, or even Martha and her frenzied fan club.

I was about two feet taller than Celso, who was a really dark-skinned kid, and was driving in for an under the hoop hook shot when he set his feet and then pounded me on the chest, knocking me down. When I called him for a foul he started cussing, "Quiere combate gringo? Quiere pelear, jodido, wanna throw blows?" and then he lit into me with a couple of haymakers. Soon, mixing tears and blood, I was flailing my arms windmill style hitting him on the back of his head and his shoulders and kicking him wildly, aiming for his nuts.

Seems like only minutes later I found myself in the principal's office more upset about the blood on my nice yellow sweater-vest and white dress shirt, and what Herbert and my parents would say, than the certainty that the paddle board was soon to descend from the wall behind the big office desk with the "Aaron Acosta, Principal" nameplate staring me and Celso in the face.

With the opening of the door came the questions, "Who started this, fellows? And Why? Anything to say? You first, Davidson?"

Mr. Acosta wore huge horn-rim glasses with extra thick lenses, so heavy and massive that they often slid down the bridge of his nose seeming like they were trying to harass his bushy black Pancho Villa mustache. Everyone called him Tio Feo.

"He did, the gringo, going around hitting my bros and yelling insults at retarded girls. He thinks he's special so I brought him down to my size!"

"What's this Strayhope? What's he talking about, bringing you down to size? You're twice as tall as Celso here!"

"I don't know sir...just trying to make a basket and he flattens me. My brother-in-law says I've got to defend myself and stand up to beaner bullies."

"None of that kind of talk, young man. I know a bit more about what goes on around here than you two bozos think—the ditch, the cafeteria, and the restrooms. And I really don't want to say more than this. If you get into any more trouble this semester it'll be more than a few ass swats. "Sabes tu? Understand?"

§

The whacks didn't hurt all that much and I explained away my bloody sweater and shirt easily enough as just a collision on the court—which it was, at least partially. I was sticking up for myself and was smug about that—until.... As things got worse with stares and threats and drawings on my locker, and trips when I'd have to march up to the front of the room to be disciplined by Mr. Montaño, a Medieval master of torture, who masqueraded as a history teacher and who had perfected squeezing you hard in a vice lock on the back of the neck and forcing you to kneel by the side of his desk, I was just about to give up all hope when, thanks be to heaven, Eddie "Q" comes back to town in all his Los Angeles suave, "firme," true pachuco swagger.

I didn't know what all the commotion was about at first. A larger crowd than usual at lunchtime was pulsing out of the main schoolyard heading for Dora Street and seemed to be congregating at the fence line that separated our school from the elementary school, both schools located on the same dead end street. End of the day dismissal saw crowds like this, what with busses and station wagons and motorcycles lining up to take students home. But this was noon and we only had thirty minutes to either go to the cafeteria or eat a sandwich under a diseased elm tree.

Was it Martha Goss maybe performing again, drawing such a crowd? There was no cheering or yelling, just a den of voices, Spanish, English, a kind of Valle del Sur Babel. It was magnetic and I just had to see what was causing all this. Apparently teachers hadn't got wind of it, at least not yet. There were no rules about staying on the grounds for lunch. Lots of people walked up to Isleta Road to the little Mushroom corner store for cokes and chips and snacks—stompers, pachucos, girls and boys.

Soon I saw the object of everyone's attention. It was the coolest of cool cars—a 1935 black Ford sedan, with bright green wheels and shinny hubcaps, all polished to a glistening shine. It sat unusually low to the ground at the front, with the rear end angled up like it had been partially hoisted four or five turns by a jack. I could see that the license plates were from California. And everyone was milling around pointing and touching the fenders and the windows, and a really tall, heavy-set pachuco guapo was kind of half heartedly asking people to look and admire but not to spoil, smudge, dent, or damage. I could see he wore black peg-leg corduroys, sharp pointed, Flamenco looking boots, and a stylish wine-colored jacket with the words "Vatos Esperanza" embroidered on the back and what looked like Aztec symbols. Two older heavily made up girls with inch-thick mascara were at his side wearing short tight skirts and sweater-like tank tops brimming over with the most shapely, luscious melon breasts one could hope for. While these "wisas" leaned against the back of the car filing their nails and popping their chewing gum, the owner-driver of the car looked up, saw me and yelled out in a guitarron voice, "Ése bro, Rory! Yo soy Eddie, Cinco Q, su vecino. Qué tal compadre, qué tal?"

Yes, he was talking to me and motioning for me to come over, which I did only to be greeted by un gran abrazo and the heartiest, flashiest handshake, from the palm to the back to palm again. Eddie had changed beyond belief and you could tell everyone who looked up to him now looked up to me because of Eddie Q's approval. How he had made such a metamorphosis was beyond me. But what really floored me was he asking me to get in the "coache"—with me riding shotgun and the girls slithering into the tufted and pleated back seat.

"Tu tiene hambre? Vamanos over to the Lota Burger for a little comida hamburguesa, cuate."

The car purred like a cat and he said he had some "Gato Negro" tomcat mufflers on it. The necking knob had a naked lady imprisoned in it and the horn when he honked it played "La Raspa." He introduced me to Yolanda and Carmelita and they ruffled my hair and squeezed my hands and gently scratched my neck with their long-nailed fingers. As we drove east for a hamburger I saw Chickie and Manny standing off to the side with expressions of deep disbelief and, dare I say, envy. Larry had one hand cupped over his balls and the other one throwing a finger, and Martha was puckering up and licking her lips as she lifted high and squeezed both breasts with her hands. Celso Davidson had turned his back and was walking away, and Tommy Newberry was laughing and giving me two big thumbs up!

After a while Eddie drove me back to school and said he was just back for a visit since he now lived permanently in L.A.—"and not Lower Albuquerque, buey," he said. When he pulled in and parked in front of the flagpole to let me out, there was Tio Feo, arms crossed and frowning, even more goggle-eyed than before.

"Pays to have influential friends, Strayhope," was all he said, accompanied by the fading melody of those special horns, and even he raised his hand to wave goodbye to a hero. As for me, I hummed "La Raspa"—now my favorite tune en todo el mundo! And I yelled as my Cinco Q vecino drove low and slow up the street, "Oralé, carnal, oralé! Hasta soon, ése bro!"

Trophy Girl

"Tail red, license light, required after July 1st 1953."
"Two headlights required twenty-four inches off ground after 1953."
—New Mexico Statutes Annotated, 66-3-804, 66-3-805

Cruising west in his swanky but exhaust-spewing 1955 powder blue Oldsmobile convertible, straight off his dad's used car lot, thankful for the quart of Bardahl motor additive and, with the sun directly hitting his Ray-Ban Wayfarers, Leo Gibbs, Rory Strayhope's and Milo Mackey's young friend, saw her waiting for the bus outside the Piggly Wiggly.

Leo knew her work schedule well by now since he passed this way often heading to Nine Mile Hill to blow the carburetor cobwebs out of his father's inventory of cars—especially old coupes and sedans ready for their inevitable transformation into race cars to be banged, bent, and wrinkled like tinfoil beyond any showroom or dingy dirt lot display.

"Yes, right on time. Can't afford to miss that 'Downtown' bus Miss Celia. But today, girl, you'll get a ride home that will change your life, courtesy of Leo!"

He'd seen her at school off and on through the year, bouncing up the stairs to the library or off to gym in her green shorts, or out in the patio at noon sharing a sandwich and a coke with Ernesto. It was there that he singled her out for his scheme. She was always in a rush and he didn't want to approach her, not with Ernesto around, and he always was around—school, work, or play—always Ernesto. It bothered him that she gave any time to a pachuco. No doubt he got her the job at the grocery store and pestered her there too, since he worked as the produce clerk for Leo's cousin, Kelley, the store manager.

"Nice, clean cut girl," Leo mused. "Plain but pretty face. Makeup—

little to none, other than a pale shade of lipstick on oh so full lips. Honey blonde hair—curled at home, no doubt. Good posture and lively movement in the way she walks—no strutting, just pleasure in her self. Shapely but not too pointed 'D' cup knockers. Long, smooth legs—a little flat in the butt, but nicer body under her clothes, he was sure, than when dressed in her JC Penney's school girl blouses and skirts. Those gym shorts confirmed that."

He'd stopped at the store before, ostensibly for a bag of chips and a coke, joked around with Ernesto and some of the other help, and waited in line three and four customers deep at her register to check out and be checked out. She'd smiled back, but never much more than a routine customer smile.

He'd imagined her without her silly Piggly Wiggly apron—and always, always without anything else on too. He'd imagined her in white, really skimpy short shorts, a tight tank top, and Paris Shoe Store high heels, mincing her way over to the checkered flag to stand there at Speedway Park, running over to whatever event's winner, handing him his gold-plated trophy, and planting a kiss on the driver's cheek, or maybe even his mouth if Leo could persuade her and rehearse it right.

He was convinced that with his narcissistic charm and the right coaching, he could turn her into a stunner, a sexy, slutty-looking trophy girl—one to make his dad proud of his enterprising son, a son worthy of buying and bestowing the Speedway sponsorship of "Oswald L. Gibbs and Son Used Cars."

He'd asked his uncle Kelley, the Piggly Wiggly manager, a somewhat older guy but young for being an uncle, about her. That is, her name, work hours, address, and if she was really serious about Ernesto or anyone else.

"Listen, Leo, Celia Vargas is a sweet kid, kind of like a little sister to me, a young woman, I don't mind saying, I have a soft spot for myself, and I don't want you or Ernesto or anyone else messing her up or screwing with her, unless they want to answer to me. So you won't get any introductions or pimp services from the likes of me, especially not for a clotheshorse, stuck up promoter like you. As for Ernesto, I keep a close eye and a tight rein on that garlic-smelling fuck. Tu sabes, nieto?"

"Claro. Whatever you say, Uncle Wiggly."

§

So, this fine decision day Leo pulled up in front of a tired and foot-weary Celia Vargas, convertible top down, powder blue paint polished to a dazzling shine, dashboard gleaming, yellow-yoked upholstery inviting, radio playing KGGM hit parade schmaltz. He whistled his standard lover boy wolf call followed by, "Hubba, hubba, beautiful" and the question: "Remember me, Leo Gibbs? So how about an A&W root beer and a ride home?"

What she sees behind his over-sized sun glasses is a freckle-faced, red nosed guy with his Hawaiian sport shirt unbuttoned over a sleeveless under-shirt–a guy she'd half noticed at school, and only vaguely remembered talking to before at her register. His dingy brown hair wasn't as tamed down and glistening with hair oil as Ernesto's, what with all the Wildroot he used and all the hourly comb swipes he made to keep the curl in the front and the deep crevice in the back of his glistening duck-tail pachuco hair. Kelley couldn't keep the shelves stocked with the oily, white grooming aid. Celia thought Ernesto was nice, a cool kid for sure, just fun to be around. Ernesto, however, didn't have a convertible and the spare change to go with it.

So, adjusting her overstuffed, tattered purse and putting on her sandals, she consented, because it was hot and she was tired and the bus was late.

The door slammed. The motor revved. She reached over to lock the door and the driver's penny loafer pushed the accelerator to the floor. The rubber burned and the smoke rose as the car lunged north on Sunset road, heading for the big orange root beer barrel on West Central for a couple of frosty A&W floats and some slick salesmanship—modeled after the used car spiel of Mr. Oswald L. Gibbs himself.

She didn't say much, just gasped and swallowed the riverside air letting it play with her long hair, damp with humidity and perspiration from waiting in the sun. The Russian olive trees were in bloom along the Bosque and their sweet aroma added to her "God's in his heaven" feeling—much better than any crowded bus ride. She inhaled deeply and leaned back into the seat while they rocketed past the Sagrado Corazón Retreat House, nestled far back in cottonwoods and surrounded by moat-like aromatic alfalfa fields.

Soon, all too soon came the siren whine of the New Mexico State Police, stopping it just as the Olds approached the bridge. "Jesus Shit

Christ! Not again! Won't that son of a bitch ever let me alone?" Leo roared.

"Up to your old tricks I see, Gibbs. Still out to set a record for the most speeding tickets in the shortest period of time? Clocked you at sixty-five in a twenty-five zone. You know the routine. This one will cost you."

And as the writing started, not forgetting his training and manners came the words, "Sorry to inconvenience you miss, but you're on a devil's ride with this obnoxious kid. Hope we don't meet up again under sorrowful circumstances."

Nodding to the blushing passenger, the young daredevil driver made a sassy introduction: "Meet the new Speedway trophy girl, Duane. She'll be out at the race track kissing the winners before you catch me again."

"Well, here's another trophy for your personal collection if there's any room in that glove compartment. File it under "L," for loser! Good luck to you, trophy girl!"

§

The recruitment proceeded through the soothing froth of root beer once they made it to the giant wooden orange barrel of a stop. As expected, the sales job succeeded convincingly and the needy and seldom honored girl, licking a sweet foam mustache from her lips, began the psychological and sartorial makeover: new cosmetics, new skimpy clothes, and a simple script needing little memorization or rehearsal.

The next introduction came loud and crackly over the public address system that very weekend. There were six small trophies and one large one—with six cheek pecks and one very bad breath mouth kiss. "Congratulations for being a Speedway winner!" And that was it, and a $50.00 check for an afternoon's work, more than a week's salary at the Piggly Wiggly.

Plus, Leo's tongue-tingling kisses were nicer and so were the flowers and the praises and even listening to Leo being congratulated for making such a find, seeing such potential, realizing the benefits of discovering, beyond imagining, just what was inside that bra and under that cheap pleated skirt.

Rides out to the West Mesa, underneath the distant dazzling stars, listening to Al Tafoya's late night radio, parking in the remote shadows of the volcanoes, seeing an occasional meteor or maybe a much rumored flying saucer—it all put Ernesto's school-yard lunches and movie dates to shame, and Kelley's avuncular supervision trailed into boredom and her decision to quit the Piggly Wiggly. She'd graduate soon and in the meantime she could cruise over to Lionel's or Bob's after school and smooch, ordering whatever sesame-coated delight she pleased without worry.

"Congratulations for being a Speedway winner!" she kept repeating and convincing herself each morning when she awoke and looked into the mirror at her newly minted sexy self.

Easy street, the big time was here, with even bigger promises from Leo to get her to prance around between rounds at Armory wrestling matches and prizefights, shaking pompoms and other things. There was even a modeling contract in the works to do Maloof beer commercials and most of all do full page ads in the "Journal" and on television for the family car lot.

"Come on in and meet Miss Speedway. Has she got a trophy of a deal for you!" went the spiel and then the throwaway kiss, which soon she was doing up in grand fashion at the Speedway. The crowd loved it. "And a kiss for you too!" she'd say over the P.A. and then toss a double handed kiss into the stands, holding an oversized papier-mâché trophy high in the air.

Soon she was everywhere, even on billboards, and not just in the city—but on the outskirts too. Every time she and Leo would drive out through the canyon over to Cedar Crest, or west to Grants and a night in the family cabin at Blue Water, and maybe a weekend at the movie star frequented El Rancho hotel in Gallup, there would be the "A kiss for you too" billboards.

It was all over whelming. Some of the attention wasn't pretty—not the late night dirty phone calls asking for all kinds of vulgar acts, some promising her a ticket to perdition. Kelley reluctantly wrote her last paycheck. Ernesto faded fast, a love to hate turn around which, she suspected, had him or his hermanos at the other end of the telephone harassments. Kelley warned her that she was playing with fire and that fame was fickle but mercifully added that she always had a job there at Piggly Wiggly if she needed it. Or if she ever just wanted to talk, she knew the number.

§

Just about the time she was ready to graduate and leave her small but cozy home, just off Edith street, and move out into the ever expanding promises of the larger world, including sharing Leo's new loft apartment in the Heights, a night of celebration overturned her cornucopia of blessings.

"Hey, a forty-nine Merc, all souped up, came into the lot this week. How about a ride out to see the stars on the mesa, have a couple of brews, and see if we can make it to the bottom of the Hill faster than any Olds Ninety-Eight, Coupe de Ville Caddy, or flat-head Ford ever could?"

"Why not? I'm a damn graduating senior and life's for living and living is for commencing!"

The car was loud, seemingly all motor, and they made it to the volcanoes almost before she could roll down her window.

"Some car, eh Babe! Never seen one with more get up and go. Real power here. This baby roars like a lion."

Once parked in their favorite spot with the city lights mirroring the dancing stars, Leo revved and raced the motor with true appreciation and then shut it down—one arm out the window, the other one cuddling her along with a bottle of Coors—and fell into his lover boy line:

"The moon's not over the Sandias yet but just imagine...those stars don't even exist. They've already burnt out. And you see that red star, that's really a planet. Mars! I'd like to zoom up there one day in a real rocket. And you've heard about Sputnik, I guess. Means 'traveler' in Russian you know. Fast bastard! And consider our government's weather satellites? Really spy satellites against the Ruskies and Gooks. Well, if we look real close we might see one. All those heavenly bodies travel faster than Einstein could calculate all his chalky numbers and equations. And speaking of heavenly bodies, let's get down to business as usual here on mother fucking earth."

After they were finished, and the empty bottles tossed with a sandy thud out into the darkness of the mesa, Leo turned on the ignition, and the motor belched awake with a rhythmic, fuel-guzzling growl.

"No flying saucers tonight, Babe, just flying long necks. And, pronto Tonto, we're off and away!" he burped. "Hold on tight, Celia, cause down we go."

Celia was groggy and still struggling to fit back into her bra, but alert enough to be scared, knowing something didn't feel right, that the car was vibrating and somehow moving of its own will.

"Leo, it's too darn dark! Aren't you gonna turn on the headlights? How can you see the road?"

"I go by the light of the stars and the moon my dear. Moon light is best for romancing and racing!"

"But there's no moon tonight! Goddamn it, Leo, you better turn on the headlights or I'm never coming out here to this godforsaken tumbleweed, cactus-strewn, broken bottle mesa with you again. Never!"

§

And, of course, she never did. The Mercury, with the speedometer needle bouncing off who knows what far-right number, tail-ended an old rattletrap pickup with no taillight, no brake light, and only one headlight. Just an old man who was lazily thinking about the state cop who just that morning gave him a warning ticket and chewed him out about the need to bring his jalopy up to inspection.

Yearbook

"It would be so sweet when all alone I'm dreaming
Just to know you still remember me."
—Scott Wiseman, "Remember Me When the Candle Lights Are Gleaming"

Larry Yeager was a real dipshit! He was a banker's son and a three-year letterman in every sport in the yearbook. I thought he was ugly as the devil with his gap-toothed Alfred E. Newman grin, his sports-frame glasses, and his cow-licked, crew cut, little round head I always wanted to use for flies and grounders.

I never did like him but what did that matter? He liked himself a lot. And so did all the girls. Well, maybe not ALL the girls, but Darlene Hopkins certainly did and to me she was pretty much ALL the girls.

I was able to take Darlene out a couple of times before I had to endure a double date with her and Larry. Don't get me wrong. I went along with them just to be close to Darlene. She'd let me get pretty close to her already, but that was before letterman Larry Yeager. He'd probably made it all the way to home plate and scored a touchdown to boot while I was preparing to bunt just to get to first base.

It was Darlene's idea...me coming along on the double date, I mean. "Oh, Ronnie," she said one night on the phone, calling me up, I first thought just to say how much fun we'd had at the old Boris Karloff horror movie. I remember that night at the Kimo leaning over and whispering in her ear while I grabbed what turned out to be a handful of dry as bones unsalted popcorn, "That monster guy looks a lot like Larry Yeager."

I meant it as a way of saying how damn ugly he was. But she just said, "Yes, he's so...manly!"

I should have got the hint, known I was striking out, figured out something was wrong right away because in my opinion you can't find a spookier looking movie star than old Boris Karloff. He even speaks spooky!

Besides, my name isn't Ronnie, its Rory. She called me Ronald once before too, and once she even called me Roy when we were snuggling, which I rather liked, to tell you the truth. It had a cowboy air about it, like I was riding with the Sons of the Pioneers or something and not sitting on her couch.

Darlene's nominal confusions and christenings were, after all, a small price to pay to get close to her. She was stacked...and you might think, given her problem with names and all, that she was ditzy. Not so. She was smart, really smart, and a member of the National Honor Society. So she came by wearing that little gold pin honestly. In addition, she had a good voice, not to mention good lungs, and she sang in the choir across town at the Fruit Avenue Baptist Church. Both at school and at church she was everybody's darling. That seems entirely understandable since Darlene probably means darling if you were to look it up. Which is what I wish Darlene had done with my name—look it up and remember it.

"Robert," her phone call continued, "I was wondering if we could go out on a date to the Halloween Hayride the Debs are sponsoring next Saturday night at Gretel Schneider's house up in Corrales?"

"Sure thing," I said. I was so pleased by the invitation I didn't want to correct her this time, calling me Robert and all. There's more than one movie star named Robert and I don't have to name them all for you. Robert Wagner is my favorite Robert. He's much better looking than old Boris Karloff. Admittedly Robert sounds like Rory, and I prefer Robert to Ronnie or Ron. When it came to Darlene I could always let something slide, if you know what I mean.

Rory John Strayhope is a rather obscure name I must say. However, I never had much trouble with it, thinking it rather down-home sounding. I always cast myself in cattle rustler type movies with a name like that. You might think of me as more of a Rory Calhoun type. Shit-faced Larry Yeager's more like Lon Chaney, Jr., the Wolf Man, or one of those sharp-toothed, fang-hanging Gothic villains like Bella Lugosi who's even creepier than Karloff.

I didn't quite know whom Darlene meant to identify by the name of Gretel Schneider. Maybe a German spy or cabaret singer like Marlene Dietrich. Although I didn't quite trust Darlene with names, that name could have been accurate since I didn't know everyone Darlene knew. She walked on the sunny side of the street you might say. I did know that Corrales was a high-toned, wealthy suburb, with some acreages and rancheros worth more than even the Simms and Dietz farms out on Rio Grande Boulevard or the Honorable Clinton P. Anderson abode off Isleta Road.

I always pictured myself owning a small but well-tended place in the North or far South Valley where people would say things like "Hubert and I are going to be at Rory Strayhope's house for the weekend out on Rio Grande Boulevard. Here's the number of his casita."

Living on a boulevard or a Blvd., as the abbreviation goes, was more my style than my parents' small acreage, although our house was more than comfortable and quite respectable for our neighborhood. "R. J. Strayhope" was more of a rancher kind of name. "Road," become "Street," become "Boulevard" would more or less signal my rise in social standing—that' s pretty much how I imagined my address changes through the years. I knew enough to know that this Gretel might well have owned an entire road, though. You don't go on a hayride down or up the boulevard.

Darlene lived on a lane, which should have told me something right away. Her little cottage of a house, or maybe it was a bungalow, was in such cramped surroundings that I backed into two mailboxes and an ornamental birdbath just turning around that first date when we went to a movie called "Shane." It was some "adult western" Darlene said where Alan Ladd plays a "conflicted gunfighter confronting the larger questions," as she previewed it. I thought it was supposed to be a comedy about some guy who embarrassed himself and was ashamed, thus "Shane." I was wrong as usual. I knew Alan Ladd wore elevator shoes and was probably ashamed of that, especially when kissing taller actresses. But what do I know about highbrow movies and Darlene's brains? She chose this movie and the "no salt please" popcorn and declined every red-hot I offered her. Jack Palance as the gunfighter saved the night for me and was my invitation to follow up with that horror movie I mentioned.

There were signs, however, of Darlene's dwindling memory. All I could see, though, was how stacked Darlene was. How well endowed she was with looks and popularity and brains and, well, a good nature. Yes, I know, as if all those things are possible in one person. Every one agrees that the quest for the total person is a worthwhile endeavor and associations do rub off, usually.

Like I say, Darlene was shapely, really stacked. "How stacked?" you ask. Better than an Egyptian pyramid I would say, much better. Although I never did know just how pyramids were built and stacked, having never seen a pyramid except in old National Geographic magazines. It's just that their shape appeals to me all pointed and everything. Stacked better than Aunt Jemima pancakes. Let's just say Darlene is round and firm and fully packed like a Lucky Strike, though she didn't really look like a cigarette, don't get me wrong—except maybe a dancer inside a package of Old Gold's.

I wanted to ask her who the Debs were too, but assumed she meant the Hi-Y club of debutante-like girls at school and not some relative of Eugene Debs who we read about in history class, or some girl named Deborah nicknamed Debbie like in Little Debbie pies and such. I would have liked to stick my thumb in Larry Yeager's horny Christmas pie and pulled out his plum, though. As for Darlene...we'll just say she was no Aunt Jemima and no Little Debbie. She was just the "oh so amazing" Darlene Hopkins.

During our fateful phone conversation I was trying to imagine just how great this Gretel girl could be when Darlene let go with a sucker punch, "You could take Joan Thompson. She's back from, you know, having her abortion and all at her aunt's place in Kansas City."

I didn't know who the hell Joan Thompson was either, or anything about her abortion. I held back on the "Say that again, Darlene!" I wanted to blurt out something like "No way, José!" Besides, I was still staggering from the realization that Darlene wasn't asking me to be her date on the ritzy hayride. She'd no doubt asked Larry Yeager. Just call me Rory Hayseed and be done with it! I felt like saying into the receiver, though all that came out was "Oh" and some flibbertigibbet noises.

And then she confirmed it, "Sweet Larry Yeager is taking me, Ron, and he'll be driving. We'll pick you up first at about 5 pm so you'll be able to do the gentleman thing and go up to the door for Joan. My mother told me just tonight when I was wondering who to call, 'Well, Darlene, I think you should ask that boy who backed into the birdbath. He was quite courteous in his apology. Just don't let him drive.' My mom's a real judge of character you know."

I was certain now that dear Darlene wasn't just sipping cognac while reclining on that couch in a rose-colored negligee as I had first imagined. Nope, she'd gone straight for her brother's model airplane glue! But then her mother seemed just as confused about me—unless she wanted Darlene to recommend me as an anonymous birdbath brain who could keep a secret.

What really burned me was to be called "the birdbath boy!" But then "consider the source" like my grandmother always said. Mrs. Hopkins had this yappy little schnauzer named Phoebe that you knew right away you'd better pet and make over and talk silly to even if you'd like to remove that damn dog's batteries and kick the curly hairball right out some dormer room window. That's where Darlene's bedroom was, up a stairway and that meant being nice to the yappy-mouthed menace... and to that dog too. If you want to know what Mrs. Hopkins looks like just think of Bert Lahr...when he played himself! Mrs. Hopkins collected commemorative plates too. And I had to see them all and imagine that Darlene might well look like her mother some day. Niagara Falls on the Fourth of July was Mrs. Hopkins' big deal favorite plate!

Who the hell was Ronnie? Who the hell was Roy? Maybe Yeager had a double your pleasure, double your fun set of twin brothers for all I knew. I soon reluctantly attributed it to demented Darlene when she and Yeager pulled up in front of my house to pick me up and take me to greet Joan Thompson. Yeager was driving this yellowish-brown station wagon with oxidized paint and fake wooden panels which suited his family name and he introduced himself to me as "Lawrence Yeager, Sport, but just call me Larry."

As if everyone didn't know who Yeager was, now I had the privilege of knowing what his friends and family called him. That was one inner circle I wanted to be out of. Next thing you know he'd be calling himself Lawrence of Arabia and that Peter O'Toole was his goddamn uncle or cousin or something.

"Larry, this is Ronald. Tell me your last name again, please."

"Rory Calhoun, star of stage, screen, and Broadway" which I thought was a good retort since our high school was located downtown on Broadway near Huning Heights.

"Oh, sure, how could I forget that? Larry, this is Rusty Nichols. He's a sophomore, maybe you knew."

"Rusty Nichols!" That was it. Darlene was hopeless. As for Darlene's mother and her endorsement of me as a good date for Joan Thompson, well an endorsement from her was as desirable as a left-handed compliment from William Fucking Buckley, another creepy guy, even more off the map that Boris Karloff, Bella Lugosi, Jack Palance, and even Alan Ladd. But hey, it was Halloween!

§

The ride out to the hayride was the stuff of a horror movie though. I don't mean to be unfair to poor Joan Thompson and her travels and travails. Why I submitted myself to such torture though, there in the back seat just to be close to the back of Darlene's blue-veined neck, I'll never know. Before it was over though I came very close to taking a bite out of her oh-so-white nape—and maybe murdering Larry, burning the car, surrendering to the county sheriff, and pleading kidnapping, torture, and insanity!

"Oh, Strayhope, Oh, Strayhope, stand up, stand up for Jesus!" Joan was saying as I tried to list my favorite tunes and listened for the sound of music from the living hell hills while trying to drive out the goddamn musical pabulum that Larry and Darlene were cooing to.

"I mean it was so awful," Joan said in my ear, "I mean if the suction goes the other way, why it's like exploding a balloon or a watermelon. But if done right it's not as painful as a clothes hanger or a knitting needle, of course. That's what Yvonne Maldonado tried. Ugh! Suction is much safer of course, and more sanitary, but it is painful...real bad painful! Can you, as a man, a boy I mean, imagine even for a minute what it was like? I mean, what I went through—even with my aunt close by? Rory, I had to leave school, which maybe you knew. And I had to endure all the gossip and insults, which Darlene told me all about. But she never mentioned you talking about me, Rory, and that's why I said, 'Sure, I'll go out with him.'"

"Does it all start with swallowing a watermelon seed, then, like they say?" I asked just to try and bring some levity to her horrific, no-holds-barred description.

"Oh, Rory, you're so funny—that's what I like about you. Your sense of humor, your sensitivity and compassion, your understanding of what we girls face at the mercy of you men, I mean boys."

"Who was the father, then? Maybe I know him? Does he go to our school?"

"I can't tell. Our lawyer saw to that. Even with a fetus there's lots of paperwork and disclaimers and documents you have to sign, especially in two states, and Missouri is worse than here. Except that here it all has to be in Spanish too. 'Chingada,' like they say. But my parents' and aunt's lawyers took care of all that. Our family attorney speaks Spanish fluently. He's so handsome, a regular Ricardo Montalbán, you know. When he came to ask me some questions I wanted to ask him out on a date. But he is married and all business. 'Hay Carrumba!' like they say."

"Well, How about the doctor, was he cute too?" I asked, just to goad her.

"Oh no, he was an old man. But he did ask me if I wanted to see what was almost the baby, and...."

"Turn up that fuckin' radio!" I shouted up front to Commander Yeager and his name-challenged cutie-cuddles co-pilot. "That's 'That's Alright Mama,'" I screamed. It's my absolute all time favorite next to 'I'm Right, You're Left, She's Gone.' And just to think, Elvis can really move too!"

"Oh, Rory, you're so well informed about music and everything," Joan said, massaging my back and curling her finger through my belt loop. I was pulling hard against the tension of two fingers and leaning over the front seat when we pulled up to Gretel's Ranchero Rico.

"I'll just pretend," I said to myself, "that I'm the Lone Ranger and that Silver was waiting in the barn for me to give him the 'High Ho Silver Away' command."

§

The tractor was running and ready and lots of kids were sitting on the flat bed and nestling down in the straw. We all ran and jumped on, and I started asking around for Gretel like the dumb valley river rat I was, but everyone was already making out and drinking beer, and the big harvest moon was coming up over the mountains and you could still hear some insects sawing away in the Bosque, and I wanted to snuggle up real close to Darlene in the worst way, whether she remembered my name or not, but jealous Joan nixed that with her promiscuous desires.

Do you know what it's like to kiss chapped lips that feel like hay? Maybe it was hay I was kissing. Whatever I was kissing, I don't wish it on you. Joan liked, worst of all, to nibble not only her lips but mine!

Thirty minutes into the chomping and the ride, right when I heard Darlene say, "On, Larry, please stop, you're making my honor society pin hurt me, squeezing me like that," I turned to hungry Joan Thompson and told her that I had to jump off for a minute to bleed the lizard and, just to make my excuse legitimate, I asked scary Larry Yeager the jerk off king if he wanted to jump off with me.

"Bleed a lizard, Rory, how are you gonna catch one in the dark?" Joan asked. And I just wised off and said, "Shoot one with one of your family Thompson machine guns!" My insanity plea was gaining more credibility I could tell.

"Oh, don't be silly we're not the machine gun Thompsons."

"Ready, Sport!" Larry yelled back at me. "Let's do it, Dopey!" And I hooted "Geronimo!" Coors can in hand and we jumped off the moving wagon into the darkness, just missing being run over by the wheels.

"Oh, boys, you be careful," Joan and Darlene screamed in chorus. "You all come right back," I heard one of them say in a sexy Cleopatra voice. But instead of trampolining back on the wagon with her Antony I ran like hell back down the road, nearly breaking my neck in a rut the size of the Grand friggin' Canyon, bleeding the aching lizard as I ran. Gretel's mom, Frau Schneider, or whoever the sophisticated braless woman was back at the ranch asked me in to rest and treat my ankle. I accepted only to hobble over to the phone and call my pal Irving Kempton and soon I was out of there cruising back down the road and onto the highway, boulevards be damned, headed for a late night burger and coke at the Frontier.

"Joan who?" Irving asked. "Not Joan Thompson who transferred to Highland? She told you all that? Did she mention me at all? Say anything about who the father was?"

"Nope. Said it was illegal to reveal that. Why, do you know her?"

"No way, Jose Farrar! Just checking cause it's good to keep confidential things confidential. I wouldn't mention it again if I were you."

"Sure thing, amigo. My lips are sealed. The sooner I forget about lippy Joan Thompson the better for me."

§

I did see Darlene again in the hall and around school and still thought she really had a terrific build, who ever did her bodywork, and however it was assembled. Her never really remembering my name kind of festered over the semester and when we were all signing yearbooks out in the Quad that spring I wrote:

To Irene
Some memories come. Some memories go.
Some names you remember. Some you just don't know.
Whatever my fame, whatever my name,
As yearbooks go, your name is ZERO!
   —Refreshingly yours, Rory John Strayhope

Hell Canyon

"it is almost fitting
to die on the railroad track.

there is something about
trains, drinking, and being
an indian with nothing to lose."
—Ray Young Bear, "One Chip of Bone"

The plaza was filled with tourists, city dwellers mostly—all in a festive mood, cameras dormant, ornamented with the permit tag required by the pueblo. The sun was hot and blazing down on the adobe walls and the hard, foot-packed clay and caliche earth. There was the perfume of fall in the air, enhanced by each occasional breeze. Most of the pueblo population was dancing, waiting to dance, resting up after dancing, or selling fry bread, lemonade, pottery, and jewelry.

Had the "tourists" known more, these urban voyeurs, decked out in their gardening visors and stylized straw hats with store-bought feathers stuck in their hatbands, and with red bandannas and neckerchiefs festooning their white, sun-block skin; had they known more fully and deeply the ancient, sacred origins of the dance and the cosmic significance of the harvest; had they sensed the life forces represented by the multi-colored corn and the deer skins and antlers and the drumming; had they realized that each rhythmic beat of the leather tipped sticks striking the leather-laced cottonwood drums echoed the heartbeats of the dancers; had they sensed the sacrality of the jingling of ankle bells and the multitude of seeds jumping and colliding inside their gourd rattles; had they sensed that each bobbing head raised to the sky and bowed to the earth in time with the pulsating music was part of a prayer; had these twentieth-century time-traveling visitors known more, then they would not have yearned to photograph and capture the moment, but instead to salute and breathlessly honor the spectacle. Even the dancers, however, especially the younger ones, were thinking more of concessions and profits, of turquoise bracelets and painted pots and servings of fry bread, and of Kool-Aid and of Coca-Cola conversations between dances.

The woman, overcome by the heat and the primitive aura of the dance and the sweaty expressions of thirst in the faces of the crowd, excused herself from her husband and son, saying, "I need water and shade and I'm heading over to that lone tree," and she pointed to an old scraggly elm. She then headed to the south side of the plaza, a good two hundred yards directly across from the white-stuccoed, ancient adobe church with three evenly distanced cross-topped spires.

She mostly saw shimmering human figures, all white with black circles painted under their eyes and dots stippled down their cheeks, as if they were crying onyx tears. She worked her way through the congestion of people, men, women, and children lining the plaza. She thought that she might faint among all the heat waves and smells of perspiration, and all the rubbery visages. She paused only to veer sharply left or dodge right and wipe away the little beads of sweat glazing her forehead and cheeks.

When she finally reached the tree she uttered, "Thank God, or the gods, as it were," and leaned hard against the rough bark, paying little notice to the pygmy black ants traversing the trunk's magnified hills and canyons. Soon the din of cicadas penetrated her consciousness and she dozed as the humming sound merged with the throbbing drums and the shimmering mirages.

Then as if out of the heat and the drumbeats and the incessant dancing feet came the voice of a young pueblo girl. "Want to be inside in coolness? Take my hand Mrs. and I'll show you inside."

§

No customers were in the gift shop. A lull before the rush to come after the dance ended. The store was filled with well-stocked cases and shelves, floor to ceiling with rings, necklaces, bracelets and artisan goods—waiting to be sold. The largest, most ornately painted pots were on the top shelf—and the woman's eyes were immediately drawn to the largest, most striking piece: zig zags of black lightning bolts, fire within the promises of corn silk. Her eyes took in the entire room, weavings, jewelry, drums, curios—and most especially the beautiful woman, dressed austerely, all in white cotton, except for a beautiful blue apron embroidered with deer, some grazing, some running, some looking into the eyes of the beholder. The first words uttered were, "My, what a beautiful apron! It must have taken many hours of close needle work."

The young girl cleared her throat and looked up from behind the guest she was shepherding, and said, "Mother, I offered this woman some shade and refreshment. Let me present her to you. This is my mother, Dolores Olguin. Mother, this is...?"

"Mrs. Strayhope, Lavola Strayhope. What a wonderful shop this is, Mrs. Olguin, an oasis really, and I do so appreciate the chance to catch my breath and revive my spirit."

"A pleasure, I'm sure. Has my daughter taken a moment to introduce her self? I can tell she likes you and honors you by her kindness. This is my youngest, Serita, or just Rita."

"Yes, she's very thoughtful, taking a heat-stricken woman under wing like this."

Soon lemonade was in the hands of the woman and conversation focused further on the challenges of embroidering and cross stitching, and on the large white and black pot with lightning and corn tassel designs that had first struck Mrs. Strayhope's notice. And with further information about the potter, one Miguel, who happened to be Rita's brother, soon the purchase was made, as well as an off the cuff invitation to come visit in the city soon—and even a conjectured offer of employment—house work or café work, or just a visit.

§

On the drive home, Lavola cradled the prized pot carefully in her lap, still haunted by the ghost-like visages of the dancers, many of them children, that had burned their way into her mind's eye, and in the midst of telling the story of the gift shop and the pot, that is, how she came to purchase it and how she met some of the potter's family, she suddenly said, "Bobby Jess, I offered her, the Indian girl, a job, for who knows what reason, charity maybe, maybe just returning a favor of a cool drink on a hot day. However, there's something special about her and I connected with her and just feel if we give her a hand, she'll make the transition into our Anglo world, maybe already has, just fine, make something of herself in our values beyond helping tend her mother's gift shop."

"Maybe that's more than enough for her and our world isn't so grand, but sure thing, whatever you want to do. It's your café. I just eat the left over chile. Besides, I'll bet she can make good Indian chile, hot and creamy."

"How old is she, Mom, and is she pretty?"

"She's probably almost fifteen, and, yes, very pretty, but very Indian, you know, and her hair is deep black and glistening, made all the more magnificent set against silver barrettes."

In the distance, close to where the road from the reservation crossed the Santa Fe tracks, B.J. interrupted the chain of thought to ask, in a tentative, squinty voice, "Do you see that light? I think that's the train, up ahead, maybe the Santa Fe Chief? The crossing is dangerous. It's the spot where a whole school bus of pueblo kids were killed. They said the bus driver was at fault—a guy from Peralta who drank more than he watched the tracks. He was killed too. Bodies everywhere. They called the pueblo governor and the priest from the church and it took hours of blessings and identifications. The whole pueblo turned out to mourn late into the night. The mystery was that there were twenty kids on the bus, twenty-one with the driver. But only nineteen complete bodies were recovered."

"How could that be, dad? Where did the others go—or the parts of them?"

Rory's question went unanswered for a moment as they stopped at the crossing to let the California Limited zoom by, and soon both mother and son were lost in their own Doppler reveries about just what Rita's move to town would mean to her, and to them.

"Hell Canyon," or so the story goes," Bobby Jess, still envisioning the carnage and thinking of massacres and genocide, finally attempted to answer his son.

§

Rita's housekeeping talents were laudable, keeping her brother's beautiful pottery well dusted and deserving of its prominence on top of the television, next to the ornate custom bound maroon and gold buckram family bible. She was given a room off the main living quarters and soon promoted to waitress in the café. After a few shy attempts at meeting customers and taking orders, she took hold and her sincerity and naturalness opened the way for acceptance by the regulars. She wore her beautiful embroidered aprons and turquoise jewelry, and worked diligently. She awakened early and often watched TV with the family or Rory before heading off to her room to read or sew or sleep, always by eight. She would routinely leave a small pan of her special chile on the stove for Bobby Jess to warm up when he came home from the station around nine or ten.

Rita's parents came to visit her and see how things were going after a few weeks, and they brought gifts. To Mrs. Strayhope, Rita's mother brought two aprons, one blue, and one gray. To Mr. Strayhope, Rita's father, Augustine, brought a large Hopi silver bolo tie he had traded for, and to young Rory they brought a large, primitive-looking Navajo turquoise ring, encircled in its brilliance with small silver beads.

Everyone was overjoyed and Rory was beside himself with gratitude. "This is a real Indian ring," he said. "I can tell."

"You have good eyes and a good heart, boy. Yes, this was given to me by my wife and Walter Begay, a Navajo friend. I'd asked him for a replacement ring for the ring I lost when I lost my finger. And when he gave this ring to me, over by Gallup, he said I could wear it for a time but it was meant for someone else, that eventually it would find its true owner."

"It's not just a pretty piece of jewelry," Walter said. "It's a ring, designed to bring bravery in the hunt and health and wholeness to its wearer. Walter says the ring too is hunting for its destiny."

"Can we go deer hunting with it, down were you live, on the reservation?" Rory asked.

"Why...of course. We'll invite you to hunt with us, me and my sons, when next hunting time comes. We'll have to decide if we should take you into Hell Canyon, though, about fifteen miles into the mountains at the far eastern end of the reservation. Some strange activity up around there though, secret military bunkers, lots of government fences and 'no trespassing' signs where the government land butts up against ours. But, that's where the deer are—and many ghosts, most recently the ghosts from the train wreck! Sometimes up there you shoot a deer and it just keeps on going. You know you made a good shot—lungs, or heart, but the deer keeps running. No blood. Nothing. Sometimes even the ravens, lions and lobos come, smelling a carcass, only to find nothing! Sometimes all you see are shadows, all you hear is the wind."

"You mean the deer are the ghosts? Or are there people ghosts up there too?" Rory asked, his eyes enlarging, his hand heading for his open mouth."

"Both animals and people. It's a place of echoes and shadows, a place to prove your courage, stand strong, and see how much heart you have. You've got that special ring, don't forget and unless one of the ghosts wants it, whatever power Walter's ring has is yours to try out for the keeping. I still search for my lost ring there—and my missing finger."

§

Late that summer another kind of invitation came—an invitation to a funeral. Rita hadn't told anyone at the café about her mother's cancer. Only when she said she had to go home and that, "My mom died and I hope you can come to her funeral in three days," did Mrs. Strayhope know.

"Why, Rita, we're so sorry. Of course we'll be there." So Bobby Jess drove Rita home to help make preparations. Then, the next Friday, everyone found themselves in the procession from the old church down the winding dirt road to the cemetery. Rita's mother was dressed in her ceremonial clothes—white blouse and leggings—and, her best red apron. Her hair and face were covered with a beautiful silk scarf and she wore a red, white, and green woven sash, securing her shawl. A pine plank with latigos was her coffin and Rory kept thinking that the body would roll off at ever turn and bump as the six men carried her to her grave. Her two sons and Serita followed in ritualized rhythm. Led by Augustine, husband, father, and pueblo official.

There was much crying and some loud, sustained wails as the hundred or so people paid last respects. At the grave, ropes lowered the plank, and shovels full of clods and dry dirt soon covered feet, waist, and face—her entire body buried. There was a scripture reading by a Catholic priest, and some native words of goodbye by a religious elder and the pueblo governor. Family and elders tossed pine boughs into the grave. Teardrops were fast absorbed in the graveside dust.

Food was at the ready when the Strayhopes arrived at Rita's house where her relatives and her newly adopted city family consoled her. Augustine introduced his two sons, Miguel, the potter, and Anthony, a much-respected weaver, and talked to them about taking Rory on a deer hunt some time in the future.

That future hunt wasn't long in coming—a future that soon became an unforgettable living past for Rory.

§

Hell Canyon was at the far eastern end of the reservation, well into the mountains. Once there, Augustine spoke first in Tiwa and held the buckskin pouch up toward the sky. His large blood-dark hand was missing a finger and his holding of the pouch was at once strong and awkwardly beautiful. On his second finger he wore a beautiful ring. The square stone of black petrified wood was polished smooth and encircled by silver beads seamlessly soldered, three to a side. Then with his curiously deformed yet somehow dancing fingers he slowly opened the leather drawstrings, holding one in his large, straight, white teeth—just like he was opening a cloth bag of smoking tobacco, ready with thin translucent paper to roll a sacred smoke.

He and his ancestors had done this outside of time and had sprinkled the small shreds in the thin paper and then lovingly licked the edges of the paper in a kind of ritualized expression of cosmic love. It was easy to imagine him back with the ancients preparing special tobacco, perhaps an ancient, decorated stone pipe, inhaling the wild weed, then exhaling and blowing the smoke clouds up toward the sky.

Augustine Olguin was a giant of a man, a Native American elder, towering over the boy with an at once intimidating and tender presence of blood and muscle and bone. His words were music with mysterious meanings, invocations, prayers of power and of supplication, prayers of the hunt arcing back to the singer's own boyhood when listening to his father's or uncle's words that paid his respects to the animal gods, and to the deer waiting in canyon forests to heed the call, to cooperate in the fleeing and finding, in the bounding jumps into the freedom of death.

The boy focused on the cloud-soft, tan, fringed pouch made all the more compelling against the blue sky—a cerulean sky decorated and sublimely accented, or so it seemed, by the dark oiled leather belt cinched by a glistening silver, sand-cast belt buckle shaped into an oval and accented by a rough-cut turquoise stone set in the very center of the buckle, a brilliant blue-green planet in a rich silver orbit—a twin to the boy's gift ring. The buckle, Olguin's wine-red wool shirt, the blue sky, the ring, and his musical words—his strange humming and staccato stuttering to ghost drums encompassed everything—combining, converging into one world of image and sound echoing order through the boy's brain and across the deep canyon where Olguin's sons stood, north side looking south. And the boy curiously knew bone deep in his not knowing. He knew he would remember this his whole life. Yet little did he know how vast and mysterious an event was about to happen and how, be it on earth, in heaven or in hell, it was to stay with him always.

When the pouch left the sky and the man's lips, and seemingly lowered itself motionless to rest beside the man's plentiful waist, tethered momentarily to the buckle and colorful Pendleton shirt, it was filled with a yellow, fine-grained powder, a bed of corn meal out of which two habitually accommodating, now fumbling fingers fished a chipped and carefully crafted arrowhead, carved, or so it appeared, out of a chip of bone or indigenous rock similar to what lay under their booted feet. Deer had been plentiful in this canyon for there were many tracks and many pellet droppings—little dark, bean-like whorls of transformed energy.

Olguin took the arrowhead and waved it in a wide arc across the sky—first to the east, then back to the west, then to the north and back in another arc to the south. Then he closed it in his hand and lightly drummed four times on his chest, over his heart.

More unknown words in Tiwa—brief words but religious, musical words, each syllable drawn out and cradled in long aspirate breaths. Then, with his strangely cursed but blessed mutilated right hand he reached over and placed the whitened arrowhead in the palm of his left hand. Then he gently placed the would-be missile in one of the larger deer tracks just a short distance from where he stood. Words were not necessary, only their sound, their intonation accompanying each choreographed action that the boy somehow understood.

Then the man spoke softly in words more familiar to the boy's ears: "We come to meet you deer. We ask you to meet us and to give us your breath, your body, your spirit. We honor you. We thank you for consenting to come to us. We dance in your path on our way. We dance coming to meet you."

And the boy followed in the short shuffling steps following the path of the deer and he knew shortly, in whatever time it would take, the deer would meet them and they would be ready and respectful for such a serious act, for the taking of the deer's precious life.

They had no clubs, no arrows, only their rifles—the man with an old but still pristine Remington .30-.06 pump, the boy with his mother's lever-action .30-.30 Winchester carbine that belonged to his mother and fitted, so she had insisted, with a customized recoil pad. When, with his mother and father, they had sighted it in out on the mesa, its thunderous retort was twice as powerful as its kick—"Gosh, hardly any kick at all!" he boasted, although his parents said, "Depends on how you hold it, son, and how many shots you take," and later that night he was surprised at the bruise on his tender shoulder.

It was a classic gun, well used and well oiled, a Winchester that had played its role in winning the West, but made more loving in its kill power by the hands of his mother who, over the last few years had shot two bucks with it, decked out in her leather fringed coat, her pale blue, silver-studded denim culottes, and her red leather mink-oiled hiking boots, a latter day heroine of her own stylized West.

It was Lavola who, with Rory's father's consent, had followed through in planning this trip with Olguin.

"Augustine," she had said, "would you show our boy the ways of the hunt down there on the reservation—the spiritual way to hunt? Show him that there are hunters and there are killers. We want him to be a hunter who kills not a killer who hunts. His father agrees and respects you as one who knows."

"Hell Canyon is the only place for such lessons. Are you good with that? Ghosts and rituals and prayers and the unknown?" Ready or not he was now there.

§

Not long afterwards the words of the big man's chant lingered in the air, rose and echoed across the canyon. Words returning from the brothers, who were on the other side, waiting for whatever, be it buck or doe, leaping or darting from the brush. The brothers yelled back across the canyon, adding to the echo still resonating from their father's song. Then, by example, the boy picked up a large rock and tossed in into the canyon, hearing it tumble off other rocks and through scrub pine and greenery he could not name.

"The deer will come to us soon—or to my sons across over the way. We must be ready."

Suddenly a high-pitched whine, more like a screaming growl came from atop a tall pine and the boy looked up to see a mountain lion stretched out on one of the top branches, head tilted back, mouth open, teeth showing, and once again came the growl from deep in the animal's throat.

"A lion up there! Look!" the boy said in a low voice. And as he readied his gun to point, suddenly, he lost his footing and toppled down an incline, twisting his ankle beneath him and hearing a branch scrunch and his leg break, and then his own echoing scream, echoing the lion's resonating growl.

Then he heard the shot, then another, both reverberating into each other, and saw the lion leap from the tree and run away, loping gracefully up higher into the canyon. And the words took form, now conscious to him:

"He's gone, but you have hurt your ankle—more than just a sprain by the looks of it. My sons will come and we will get you out. I'm going across the canyon to meet them and then we will return."

"But the lion? The deer? It hurts!"

"You have your gun. You have the pouch. And you have Walter's ring. You will be fine. Believe me when I say that we will return in an hour—no more."

§

He was alone then. More alone than he had ever been before.

And he was frightened. There were the sounds of mountain jays, the trees seemingly whispering in the breeze, and the close barking of strange tasseled-ear squirrels. Overhead in the high blue sky a hawk soared on thermal winds. Now and then ravens quarreled at a black bird. At first there was pure silence. Soon, ground sounds could be heard and it was anything but silent. There were other living things around him, but he was alone—the only human around. He gripped then cradled his mother's rifle.

His ankle hurt deep. He tried to get up and walk, using his rifle as a kind of crutch, but he was afraid of clogging the barrel with dirt. So he sat down, situating himself against the trunk of a large Ponderosa pine tree so that he could see where the lion had gone. The boy scrutinized its tracks and route of escape, thinking that any moment it would come bounding back. He made sure a shell was in the chamber, convincing himself that he could fire faster than any lion could run. He rubbed the ring and repositioned the leather pouch around his neck, feeling the cornmeal and the hardened arrowhead inside. "Like a piece of back bone," he thought.

He dozed, soon awakened by the ache in his ankle. Then he dozed again, feeling the sweat and the fever, and he saw in the near distance two children talking with a Navajo man who was leading them along the trail. Rory first thought it was Olguin and his sons...but it was someone the boys called "Water," or "Walter." The children looked like smaller versions of the man. One of them carried a brown paper lunch-sack like he had often taken to school. Another child, a little girl, had an inexpensive vinyl school satchel in her hand and she was swinging it. Walter was in jeans with a beautiful blue and white-flowered feed-sack shirt and on his finger was a huge ring with a stone of polished coral set in sand-cast silver patterned like a walnut hull.

Rory thought he heard the girl say something in Navajo, although he strangely understood what she said, "Is he alive or like us? If we take his ring, will you give it back?" And Begay was saying, "He's still alive and the ring is strong. It's making him hold on. And, no, we came to restore a ring, not to take the ring he now wears to prove his worth."

Then Begay and the children were standing in front of him. But then, in the shaded distance behind them the lion suddenly appeared but on second look it wasn't the lion...it was Augustine Olguin!

"Where did you come up with the design of that one, Walter?" Olguin asked. That's like the one cut off with my finger when gutting that ten point buck in this canyon of spirits." And Olguin held up his hand, the one with the missing finger, raised it high and pushed it into Begay's face.

"You know I trade all over. I can't be sure where everything I trade for comes from. I don't remember where I got this stone. Maybe Santo Domingo? Maybe Zuni or Acoma—but the sandstone setting is Navajo. Maybe I crafted it myself with the help of my magical parrot."

Rory tried to raise his gun to shoot whatever he could hit, but one of the children shape-shifted into Dolores Olguin and she was frantically waving a beautiful apron, embroidered with deer, like a flag of surrender so that just as Rory placed his finger on the trigger, his finger fell off in a rivulet of blood...and he swooned, thinking he had surely fallen beyond mercy into hell itself.

§

Minutes later Rory roused. However, he wasn't certain he dreamed what he had heard but he reached over and made sure he still had his fingers and his ring. It was still on his finger, which was twitching but still attached to his gun hand. The stone seemed to wobble in its mounting while the little circle of BB's was moving, rotating first clockwise then back. And he saw not one stone but two, turquoise becoming coral, coral becoming turquoise. The he realized he saw two rings on his enlarged finger, not one. One was huge and fit more like a bracelet than a ring.

A low growl made him look up to see that the lion was back, sitting casually on its haunches not ten feet away, saying to him with a yawning smile, "I've come back for you...and for your blood meat. I've devoured many an animal, deer, man, boy, and woman here and taken many souls. So I not only know all the soul flavors of all the centuries of ghosts up here, the dead of many generations—they are all part of who I am and what I'm here for. I alone rule in this canyon of the lost."

But when the boy finally had the courage and at the urging of his mother's voice to raise his gun and shoot, the woman with her beautifully wondrous apron flew to his side, saying, "I will protect you. My daughter bid me to come. Hand me your rifle so I may offer it to the lion and he will not take your ring, or your soul. And tell my husband when you see him that I came to restore what was his."

"How can I be sure that you are not just some fever spell?" Rory asked.

"I am a deer spirit, here for a short term to protect stranded ones like you even though I died and you saw me buried and returned to the earth. I live for now with the ones who barter lives. So believe what I say and live. Your only protection is your belief. If you believe the pain in your ankle, you must believe me."

§

Augustine awakened Rory, returning as he promised with his two sons, bringing water, strong young arms, and the means to carry the disoriented boy out of the canyon.

"Wait! My ring? My rifle?" And they all looked on the darkened ground to see two blemished but intact rings.

"Your wife came to protect me. She returned your ring and she saved mine!"

Olguin and his sons said nothing but looked to the sky and prayed muted words in Tiwa against the faint growl of a hot wind following them as they climbed out of Hell Canyon.

Chigger

"It's a poor sort of memory that only looks back."
—Lewis Carroll, *Through the Looking Glass*

He'd had the dream before: always the same beginning but details filling out now, brown and white, brown and white—and droplets of red. Always the same colors, always the same longing for something now more mysterious, now a kind of freedom, a release, a flight like the quail's, the young bobwhite trying desperately to escape the brush pile. It had to get out. Had to weave its worried way through the stacked sticks and brambles, its soft feathery body snagging on the hard dry branches, before the bonfires, before the conflagration, before a happening it knew to be permanent, something called death. To stay was to die. To fly was... maybe to live.

Rory stood there watching the bird struggle to be rid of its refuge and its jail, intuiting that to fly would be risky because he was standing there watching, his thumb on the hammer of his new .20 gauge, single-shot gun. He was ready. And he half hoped the quail would turn and go back into the brush pile, back into its sanctuary, its cover. Rory looked into the little shinny black eyes of the struggling, stuttering bird as it finally broke free, its brown and white mottled body no longer camouflaged by the branches and dead foliage. It was airborne in a whirr, its new wings working fast and hard and Rory raised the gun and led it just like his uncle Willard had instructed him.

And as the lead BB's hit and the bird folded in the air in a puff of softness, Rory heard the whistling and the chirping of the other quail flying from the brush..."bobwhite, bobwhite, bobwhite..." they were singing and his father, B.J., Bobby Jess, yelled out, "Hot damn! You hit it, son! You hit it! You damn well did!" And his uncle, shooting rapidly in the distance, waved to him and raised his old pump Winchester high above his head and he could see he was smiling.

Rory ran, stumbling on the rough earth, to retrieve his prize but when he bent down to pick it up he realized he was crying and when he raised the small, soft bleeding ball of feathers to look at it more closely and to wipe the tears from his eyes, a drop of blood fell in a quiet splatter on his new Red Wing boots, and another on the barrel of his new gun, the red soon turning rust color against the hot bluing, strangely merging in his senses with the smell of the gun powder. And when he broke the gun to eject the shell and reload he wished the lifeless, mechanical arch of the cartridge was bringing new motion and vitality to the warm death he held in his hands. And he knew, like the quail, he would long remember that same frightful longing of the dead bird to be flying free.

§

He undressed in the cold bedroom, feeling before really seeing the tiny red spots around his ankles and groin. Both women insisted that he take a hot bath and that he needed to get rid of any chiggers and any ticks. It was Billy Sue who ran the bath water in the big-lipped tub, and directed him down the hall, the floor cold on his feet and his arms pulled in against his chest and covering himself in a shudder. His mother, trailing behind, was laughing and remembering, asking her sister-in-law, "Do you remember your inspections and baths? Damn Okie chiggers, they were here then and they'll be here in the hereafter, that's God's good bet!"

"You rest easy Sugar, Aunt Billy Sue can see them, feel them, and pinch them in the dark."

The water was hot but felt good, cooling comfortably against his goose-bumpy skin and he held Billy Sue's arm as he stepped into the giant farm tub with rust spots where the water had been dripping over the years. It reminded him of the bloodstain on his new boots, the quail blood he had tried to wipe off first with grass and then, on the porch, with a rag while the joking between his uncle and his father continued.

"What a shot," Willard said, slapping the boy on the back. "Two birds on his first time out and with his new little gun! How many will he bag when he gets a double barrel or a pump? But who needs a fancy gun when he's got such a dead eye. 'Little Dead Eye,' that's what I'm gonna call him from now on. He just has to follow that dominant eye trick I taught him."

All Rory could really see then and still in his mind's eye with each tiny glistening red chigger his aunt found was the stain on his new boot that wouldn't wipe off and he kept seeing the droplets of blood from the poor quail's beak and lifeless tongue, never to sip cool water again, never to repeat its syllabic song.

The forceful bath water soon covered his ankles and his legs as he sat down, slipping and banging his bottom hard on the tub. He'd just gotten his balance and settled in when Billy Sue leaned over him, her full breasts popping free out of her blouse just like the quail he'd killed popped free from the brush pile.

"Oh, I see another little bastard, she hollered. Let me at it." And she reached down between his legs and brushed her hand against his scrotum and pinched at what he could now see was a chigger. "I got it good and she squeezed it hard between her fingers and he flinched, thankful she wasn't squeezing him down there, wondering even so just how that would feel.

"There's another one...and there, and there," each little red villain meeting the same fate under the forceful fingers of his bosomy aunt. Then he strangely felt himself get hard and it surfaced through the water, its head and little eye pulsing red, and his face, too, blushing in embarrassment. And he remembered again the quail's blinking eye in the brush pile.

"Oh my, Lavola, your little boy isn't so little any more," his aunt said. And his mother paused for a time, finally saying, "Guess you're right. Better give the chiggers a rest, though, and dry him off."

§

That night, well dried and with Watkins ointment soothing his bites, he cuddled under the warm quilt, almost able to see his breath in the cold air of the back bedroom and he reached down to feel his lingering hardness trying to understand what had happened and he imagined his aunt rubbing him, saying, "Is that what I think it is? It's sure not a chigger, is it, Sugar?" And the warmth of her hand and the bath water again engulfed him. Seeing again her mounded breasts and imagining their nipples he felt an urge down there. And his hand was smothered in his own milky whiteness and he fell into a deep sleep. And he was flying, flying fast out of the brush pile become his aunt's rounded breasts. And he flew across the field and into the copse of nearby trees and he was free and he was whistling "bobwhite, bobwhite, bobwhite!"

§

Rory awoke to voices and the smell of coffee and bacon and eggs. At first he didn't remember where he was, but he heard Willard and Bobby Jess talking about the day's hunt.

"Virgil says to follow the river down to the big mesa. That's where Juan saw a couple of bucks and a herd of does just days ago when he was working cattle."

"Good. You drive us down there and let us off. We'll walk up the south side of the canyon to the table top and you can shoot the whole herd when we drive them to you...those we don't drop."

And he thought of Virgil, the rugged-looking rancher who met them when the first drove up from Beaverhead and the little lake and took them into the big living room of the field stone ranch house with its corrals and old vehicles, and showed the women the way to the kitchen and the men to the bunkhouse just across the yard.

They'd met Juan too, the Mexican national working the ranch that fall and riding his blazed-faced sorrel outfitted with a Mexican saddle with an oversized pommel and hand-carved stirrups. And they'd watched him slaughter a calf, shoot it in the head and then proceed to bleed it and butcher it. "Chingada, la muerte!" he said when he cut its throat, while his nervous little border collie followed at his heel, and Bobby Jess asked in half-baked Spanish, "Donde están los venados, amigo?" Juan replied in Spanish, English, and something in between.

"Si Señores. Hay mucho venados al sur, más alla en la boca grande. Many of the deer over there. Muchísima carne y muy sabroso, muy!"

Rory had little appetite left for meat, seeing the poor calf fold up in a limp lump, never to walk or even stumble again, making its last walk down the chute aside the corral, to meet Juan and the .22 bullet through the brain he greeted it with. The women lingered in the house with Virgil, having a cup of coffee while the men grabbed the rifles and the hunting and cooking supplies, carrying them into the bunkhouse.

Awakening in the bunkhouse Rory rubbed his eyes and stretched his feet and toes remembering yesterday's breakfast in Magdalena and the desolate trip across the San Agustin Plains, then finally reaching the black range and the seemingly endless gravel road into the scrub oak and the juniper and finally the tall pines. Willard and Billy Sue had followed in the same green Chevy coup they'd traveled in to New Mexico after selling their Oklahoma farm, Billy Sue at the wheel and Willard reading a map on the passenger side. That career change had transformed Willard from a confident cattleman into a morose milkman, all for the sake of his health, in search of dry Southwestern air easier to breathe, air guaranteed to be better for his asthma. The faded green Chevy was road weary now, the paint no longer lustrous, now coated with New Mexico dust and, no doubt, regrets.

"Is this what you moved us here for?" he heard his aunt say with that edge in her voice he'd heard now for a year or two over family dinners. "Why'd we have to follow B.J. and her here? Arizona, Colorado...why not there? Tell me."

"Oh, Billy, stop your bellyaching and help me with the table. Find the damn syrup and the knives and forks. Pour the coffee for Christ's sake. Make yourself useful!"

"Arguing again," Rory thought, "spoiling what could have been a man's hunting trip into the mountains. That must be what comes of bad blood between sisters-in-law: resentment, jealousy, picking, pecking, picking, pecking." Then he remembered snippets of the dream and the softness of Billy Sue's touch back then, a touch he'd never forgotten and wished for even stronger now. He'd told himself over and over that he shouldn't think of her that way but he couldn't help it, wishing the girls in school were as alluring as her.

"Wake up Chigger, rise and shine. Get this man's breakfast into your big boy's stomach so you can bring us back some red-blooded meat."

She'd called him "Chigger" since that bath. "My way of saying Sugar, Sugar," she'd explained. He half hated yet loved the nickname and all it suggested.

"Oh, will you leave the boy alone, Billy, and stop calling him that. You damn well know his given name is Rory John so call him by his given name. R.J. is okay. Anything but 'Chigger'; that's a terrible sounding name just like...oh, the hell with it! If it means Sugar to you call him Sugar."

He was hungry for bacon and eggs but lulled in his bedroll as long as he could, self-conscious to walk until he was back to normal and able to head straight for the small bathroom without notice.

Then he heard Lavola's voice, "By the way gents, we're going hunting today or tomorrow too—our own self invitation. Virgil said he would show us some promising spots nearby if you wouldn't take us. So be prepared for a challenge from the ladies."

The men and the boy, finally at the table, laughed at their getups, especially his mother's new boots and hand made denim culottes. The whole family had gone down to Simon's and bought new boots. He'd hated to give up his old blood stained boots, but by now he'd out grown them by a size and a half. "Those old bloody boots had character, son, but can't hunt with blisters and sore feet." So he'd bought a pair of Wolverine boots with white wedge souls. His mother bought a pair of calf high lace ups and high socks. She looked like a combination of a lumberjack and a drug store dandy. So she was in hunting costume, and she'd brought her .30-.30 too and a box of silver tip Winchester shells arranged in a leather cartridge belt, causing Billy Sue and Willard to call her Annie Oakley. "Those are extreme lineman-like boots, Sis! They'll come in handy if you see a bear."

"Kid me all you like! I'll out walk you men any day of the week. And pay Billy no mind."

"Yes, you know me. No need for hunting boots—unless it's in high heels for hunting a different kind of dear. For this kind of adventure, just like Eve my oxfords will do. If I want to kill a buck I'll just charm him to death, right Chigger?" Billy Sue said, and winked at the boy.

He saw his mother glower at her with a deeper kind of anger than usual but he obligingly just said, "Right, Aunt Billy Sue, like a deer in the headlights, huh?"

§

The road south along the east fork of the Gila was more like a trail than a road and B.J. had to put the truck into compound gear, saying, "Should have borrowed Virgil's old Dodge Power Wagon for this." And between bumps and jostling the boy reached down and checked the safety on his rifle, remembering how Kenyon Jones shot his brother by accident on just such a bumpy back road. "Bullet went clean through him, through the back of the seat and out the dash. Rory had seen the bullet hole and heard the story retold more than once in warnings about gun safety.

Willard had won more than one marksman medal in the army, although he was in the Signal Corps and had never seen any real combat. He was strict when it came to guns and taking care of them and handling them. Who knew if he was thinking about his Army days when he spoke up, saying, "See that wide-mouthed canyon to the right? This is close to Juan's spot, so let me out here and I'll climb up to the table top and meet you both one canyon over."

"Me too?" Rory asked in excitement. "Wasn't that the plan?" He had wanted to hunt with his uncle rather than his father who had, at least in the boy's mind, been relegated to driving the truck and loading supplies. And when sighting in the rifles on the volcano rocks he seldom hit the target.

"No you go with your dad. More chances for success that way. And I can move faster alone."

It was his uncle who had the reputation of being the outdoorsman, carrying a big hunting knife on his belt and his bolt-action 30-06 rifle on a sling, boasting of learning how to use a sling to steady his aim in the army.

"Sure thing. Sounds like a plan. Rory and I will be waiting for what ever you drive off the mesa. If anybody gets lost, shoot three times. I'll honk the horn three times to let you know where the truck is."

The boy waved goodbye to his uncle and watched him head up the canyon. A fat tasseled-eared squirrel darted out of his way and skittered up a tree, pausing to hold a small nut in its little feet. Willard, he chuckled to remember, had told him that the best way to catch a squirrel was to "grab his nuts."

They parked the truck at the mouth of the next canyon and walked through the brush for a good distance before his father motioned to start the climb, signing to him to be as quiet as possible with the loose rocks and to secure his footing. When they neared the top, Bobby Jess spoke softly to his son: "Stay here next to this boulder. You'll be down wind if what Willard scares up comes this way. I'll go on ahead for maybe a hundred yards or so where you can still see me. Stay alert and watch for whatever comes over the mesa, including Willard."

Rory had been alone in the wilds before, but mostly along the river near his home. He'd waded the muddy water of the Rio Grande and called in ducks and even once shot a Canada goose, although he regretted it and could still hear the thud of the great bird when it hit the mud at the edge of a sandbar. He didn't like shooting birds, small or large, and he'd never forgotten the frightened, longing look of that first quail he'd shot on Willard's farm years earlier.

"They've got the first dollar they ever made and could buy us out ten times over, Lavola would always say, piling complaint upon regret, "Don't know why you don't have the business sense Willard has, Bobby Jess. Without my pestering you'd give away the store, which is just what that sister of yours will do, given time, if she doesn't leave him for another man. Billy's a damn gold digger, B.J., if there ever was one. You know it's the truth. She's a cock teaser, she is. I've seen you drool over her too, better believe it!"

"Now, Lavola, she's your sister-in-law and not as bad as all that," he said.

§

Rory sat there next to the boulder feeling its warmth and the brisk breeze hitting his face and hair, not caring about sunburn, just happy to be waiting, watching, thinking. He wondered what Lavola and Billy Sue were doing and again remembered Billy Sue touching him down there. He'd seen her flirting with his dad more than once, sitting on his lap, taking off his hat, messing with his hair, what little there was. At first he didn't realize just what was going on. He'd never seen his parents look that way—neither one of them. Billy could nestle up real close to you, touch your hand, and you'd see her bare arms and feel her breasts through a hug and you'd want to die to be in bed next to her, in his bedroll or maybe in the dark at a drive in movie...just anywhere. That's why, he guessed, she kept coming back in his dreams.

He'd seen her act that way morning and evening with Virgil, even Juan, when they first arrived and when Virgil led the way to the kitchen, where she'd made Rory a peanut butter sandwich, casually scraping the mold off the jelly, and cutting off the crust of the stale bread, and tempting Virgil with a spoon full of the hard, brown mix, saying, "It's still good. You'll see. Just try it. If you try it I'm sure you'll like it." Virgil had reached up grabbed her hand and turned the spoon back toward her mouth, saying, "You first." And she'd said, "No, no, I don't want to," and Virgil had said, "Ah, no means yes where I come from!" And just then Lavola had walked in and scolded them all for being children and misbehaving in front of Rory.

"Oh, he likes peanut butter," Billy Sue answered for him. "He knows who butters his peanuts, right Chigger?

And he'd watched his mother flush and reach for a paring knife on the counter, and say, "Goddamn it to hell, Billy, I said don't call him that, and I mean it! I'm not going out hunting with you today for damn sure."

Then Virgil stepped in, grabbing the little double-edged potato peeler, saying, "Now ladies, this is no way to start your visit with uncle Virgil. Save all that energy for the deer!"

Then Virgil turned to Rory and asked, "Why does she call you Chigger, kid? Some down home joke going on?"

And Rory remembered being too scared to say anything and just turning and heading outside, sitting on the stone fence, trembling, wondering why that word riled his mother so, and whether she would have really taken that knife to Billy Sue. He'd seen his mother lop the heads off chickens and that tails off puppies she was raising. He'd heard arguments before about how his mother and uncle had to share an inheritance and how she resented Billy Sue having any claim at all on Willard's money that she some how felt was due her. Maybe that's what was behind it. But he only knew snippets and innuendos.

§

The wind picked up but the air was light and clean and the boy wished that there was no anger anywhere, and that he had succeeded in getting that damn quail blood off his old boots, and that he could just sit there beside that boulder forever with his new boots and never have to grow up, never have to be caught in the brush pile of his relatives, free to fly like that wayward bobwhite, to ride the wind like a bandit, heading to Mexico, longing to, needing to reach some dark, dusky girl. He'd kissed Lucinda Metzger and Freddie Chavez's sister, Florinda, on the ditch bank behind his house and he was imagining that romantic moment when two loud shots rang out in the distance. It was Willard! Close but not as close as his father who, not too far away, was waiting, calmly sending up puffs of smoke from his ancient nicotine-caked pipe.

Then all of a sudden, he heard the clamor of hooves on rock, deer running fast, and over the rim of the mesa and down the canyon wall came two bucks. Big ones he could tell. Ten pointers at least! He readied his gun...took off the safely, and put his finger lightly on the trigger. His heart was beating, his eyes were watering, stinging from tears and not just the wind, and he wanted to yell to his father, but he couldn't fully see him, couldn't find him behind the scrub oak and juniper. He wasn't where he was supposed to be...no smoke. Then the bucks were in range and he heard the retorts of his father's old .30-40 Krag, "Whop! Whop!" and then he opened up, shooting blindly at the motion of the deer. Then another volley of shots from Willard's direction, "Pow, Pow, Pow!" But Rory could only see one buck! Then the dust kicked up beside him, first one bullet, then another, ricocheting off his boulder not ten yards from him. And he started yelling, "Hold your fire! Hold your fire! You're shooting at me!"

Then his father's shrill voice, "I got him boys, I got him!" he heard his father shout. "I hit the son of a bitch right in the neck. A lucky shot but I took steady aim boys. I got him!"

And then the yelling came from Willard running and stumbling and sliding down the embankment, "God damn it to hell! We're in a cross fire!"

When they made it to Bobby Jess and the buck he'd shot—or thought he'd shot, and made sure none of them had been hit, Willard said I think I got him B.J. I hit him before you saw him. Right at the edge of the mesa...."

"But look," Rory said, "he's been hit twice, a gut shot and a neck shot. Maybe you both got him. He's a beauty." And the boy's heart sank in sorrow for the lifeless creature. But, he held back his emotions, saying only, "Where's the other buck?"

"Look for blood, boy. See if you see blood where he'd been hit," Willard said. And while Bobby Jess and Willard were dressing their buck, Rory found it—a trail of blood, small pink spots, then large red splotches leading over the rocks and on out the canyon.

"Maybe, just maybe I hit him," he thought. "I'm going to follow the trail!" the boy yelled.

But his father called him back to help dress out the dead buck and carry him back to the truck. "We'll look for him first thing tomorrow, Rory. First thing. But tonight we're going to have venison steaks. So the gals better have the stove ready. We're bringing in a buck!"

§

The return to the ranch was met with celebration. Jesse started honking as soon as the corral was in sight and when Juan looked up to see what all the commotion was about

B.J. greeted him in halting Spanish. "Qué tal, Juan? Mira atrás! No tenemos hembras. Mira, hombre, mira lo!"

And Juan smiled a wide response, "Verdad? Qué bueno, güero. Qué bueno! Tù felicitas!" Juan's dog barked its enthusiasm, reared up on the truck to sniff, and followed the truck and the smell of meat up the rest of the way to the ranch house. Willard and the boy sat quietly, each of them thinking, deciding what really happened and what was true. The buck was dead, that was true. And its companion had been wounded, but was that really worth celebrating? Only in the world of hunters it seemed. Only in the world of men was such issued death special.

Soon Virgil and Lavola and Billy Sue came out of the ranch house offering their congratulations. They were nervous somehow, and Billy Sue kept fiddling with her hair. Virgil spoke first, saying, "That's a good size buck! This calls for a big dinner of fresh venison. So hang the carcass over by the gasoline pump, skin it, dress it out, and cut us some steaks. I'll get the kitchen ready and you all come to the house for dinner. I've got a special bottle of good wine waiting for this."

"Did you really shoot it, B. J.?" Lavola asked him in a whisper.

"Sure did. A clean shot, right in the neck. Willard might have hit him in the gut, but I brought him down. And we think Rory hit and wounded another one. We'll go out looking for it tomorrow for sure."

In a few hours everyone had cleaned up for dinner at the big table in the main ranch house. Toasts were made. Potatoes and some salad were served up and the fresh venison steaks were devoured and enjoyed by all, except for Rory. The meat was too rare for him, not just pink but blood red. He kept thinking of the other buck out there somewhere, either dead or suffering and his appetite waned—as did his mother's who knew something was bothering her son, thankful that he really didn't know what had transpired there at the ranch while he was out hunting. Maybe she had walked in on the flirtations become intimacies of Virgil and Billy Sue and had confronted them in a fit of disappointment and anger—reluctant to confess she was jealous, having long wondered what it would be like to be in Virgil's strong arms herself, almost breathing the words, "Always, always, Billy Sue, Billy Sue...men at her beckon call, always, always that bitch."

Suddenly Lavola spoke up, "We'll go with you tomorrow, Rory, to help find that wounded deer! Right Billy Sue? You'll go with me tomorrow. No more hanging around the ranch like today. Okay?"

And Billy Sue looked up from her second glass of pinot noir, cast an aggravated look at a grizzled Virgil and gulped a "Sure, sure!"

"I'll really get to break in my kicking boots, now!" Lavola said, with spite in her voice."

§

The two women and the boy rode in the back of the pickup—the boy sitting precariously over one wheel well and the women holding on to the cab through open windows. Bobby Jess drove and Willard sat across from him, his rifle muzzle pointed down, knowing that one good jolt might send a bullet through someone. He hadn't wanted the women to come along and was still moody about the fact that B.J. had claimed the deer he was convinced he first shot heading down the rim of the mesa. He'd give the boy the other deer, although he doubted if such nimrod shooting had really hit it. Plus, Willard was sulking because Billy Sue has passed out in bed last night in the middle of his advances.

Bobby Jess hadn't wanted Lavola and Billy Sue along either. However, he was still enjoying the fact that he'd downed that tasty, trophy buck.

Rory's mind was on the other buck he hit, sure that he was the responsible one. This killing of beautiful animals was proving less fun than he'd expected, but he had to keep up his manly appearances so as not to disappoint his father and uncle. He was, after all, one of them, one of the age-old society of hunters, and he too resented the women tagging along. He looked again at his aunt's alluring anatomy searching more intently the geography beneath her blouse, than for the canyon where they had killed B.J.'s buck. He'd leave that to his dad and uncle.

Billy Sue balanced her self well and looked at the scenery with considerable enjoyment, thinking more of Virgil and their recent rendezvous than the river and the landscape of grasses, scrub oak and juniper trees. "More like a tall pine, that man," she thought, while Lavola imagined various ways to pay her back for always calling Rory "Chigger," for her way with men, for her damn good looks, and always, always being at the center of attention. She thought Willard was reaping the whirlwind for marrying such a floozy but felt a sister's dutiful sorrow for him at the same time.

The reveries were broken by Bobby Jess's shrill words, "That's the canyon isn't it Willard? I remember dragging the buck over that bed of rocks."

"Yep. That's it. Pull over and we'll spread out and look for the other one."

No helping hands were needed for the woman and the boy who were out of the truck before the men had even opened their doors.

"Here's his blood, going this way out of the canyon and across that little meadow and then up into those smaller hills," Rory reported. "I'll follow them heading east."

The others hesitated, waiting for Willard or B.J. to make a decision as to how to fan out. Soon Rory, walking fast, gun at the ready in front of his chest, was out of sight. There wasn't much fresh blood at first, the original splotches having dried over night. But then the splotches grew larger, some even with clots. If the deer hadn't died in the night in would be a miracle. If the bullet or bullets had hit its legs it was severely crippled. If a gut shot the poor creature was in bad pain.

Rory kept walking, hesitating only to check the closeness of the splotches, paying little mind to the sky. When he looked up he was into the hills and surrounded by a dense stand of piñon and scrub oak. His hands were sweating and kept sliding on the stock and forearm of his rifle but the gun was light, almost weightless to him. Then...he saw it. Larger than he imagined! It was lying on its side, it's heavy rack of antlers holding its head in a twisted position. He walked up slowly to within ten or fifteen yards, wary that if still alive it might gore him or kick him in its terror. It was dead. He was certain. Blood no longer oozed from its nostrils. Flies were covering its dull eyes. The bullet had hit its right flank, tearing apart its hip and ripping into its intestines. He stood in a swoon over the deer, seeing again that first bobwhite quail struggling to fly free of the brush pile. And despite his efforts he started sobbing for the deer, for himself, and for that long ago, distant quail. He took off his sweaty, red-plaid hunting cap and simply said, "Forgive me, forgive them, forgive us all...." Then he silently wondered just how he had been part of such a cruel act. And he knew, knew deep inside that he would never hunt, never kill anything again.

The prayerful stillness was broken by a shot, then a scream some distance behind him. Then, minutes later, three blasts of the truck horn. When he made it back close enough to see the truck, he knew something terrible had happened. Forget about the dead deer. His father was cursing and kicking the brush. Willard was cussing and pointing his gun at Bobby Jess. A woman lay on the ground, legs and arms sprawling. She wasn't moving. At first he thought it was his mother. Then he realized it was his aunt. It was Billy Sue! Her chest was a gaping bloody hole. Her beautiful breasts had been blown away.

Then the voices and words finally sunk in, "I didn't mean it. You've got to believe me. I'm so sorry, so, so sorry!"

When Rory finally reached Lavola she was crazed, out of her head and babbling, her hands and clothes covered in blood as if she too had been shot. Her face was freckled with what reminded him of little chiggers of blood. And she was trying mechanically to wipe away the dark specks of blood from her culottes and legs with her hands. And she kept crying, "My poor Billy Sue! The safety was on. No shell in the chamber. It was an accident. An accident...."

Yellow Roses

"And as the door of love between us closes
Tears will fall like petals when we part."
—Bob Hilliard and Steve E. Nelson, "I'm Sending You A Big Bouquet of Roses"

He fumbled a bit, as usual, when he pinned on the gardenia corsage—pricking his finger as he pushed the pin through the reluctant brocaded material of his wife's dress.

"Blood!" she almost screamed. "Watch out for the blood! You never, never, learn! Why is pinning on a corsage any more difficult than unsnapping a brassiere?"

She loved gardenias and ever since high school dances, and other auspicious occasions, like this wedding for Jenny, one of his wife's girlfriends, he always saw to it that he bought Evelyn's favorite flower, always worth the price. Blood or no blood.

Roses too were that way and he remembered carrying the bouquet of yellow roses from the car to the porch and leaving them by the front door. Those puncturing, scratching thorns were much more painful and lasting than a corsage pin. Those rose pricks had lasted four or five years and brought him to remembering that past converging in this present and, no doubt, this night's memories to store up for the future. Had things worked out a bit differently he'd have bought more roses over the years than gardenias—not yellow roses and all they suggested to him about his decision, his lack of courage, his guilt for saying goodbye with a dozen paltry roses and a note—a quick delivery and a dash back to the car and a ride into another life with another woman, a woman whom had once jilted him just like he jilted Odelia. Both loves would be here at this wedding, both together, each one seeing the other, and him there in the middle of what was and what could have been—and what would be.

The bride was Evelyn's and Odelia's friend. He knew Jenny too. In fact, it was Jenny who had called him at college and spoken those fateful words, "It would be a mistake to marry Odelia, Rory. Evelyn still loves you and wants to see you one more time. Can you drive up here this weekend?"

He did drive the three hundred miles north along the Rio Grande, at breakneck speed he remembered. Now he was at another crossroads, seeing all the principals in his own little soap opera, and who knew what would be said, what he would say, given the years' buildup of guilt, embarrassment, and sentimentality. The perils of nostalgia seemed now to outweigh the pleasures.

That fireball of a drive was a bookend to other fateful drives, other personal crossroads and he thought back to that slow, beautiful, snowy drive along the twists and turns of Rio Grande Boulevard that December when he had taken her home and there on the floor in front of that old natural gas wall furnace with its orange glowing elements, all but proposed to Odelia. She was like hot snow, soft and glowing and, warm and moist and he had never forgotten how her taste and smell had so startled him in its primordial freshness.

She assumed more than was actually said, taking actions for words, kisses and caresses for an actual proposal. And he had to admit that at that time, in that room, amidst those emotions their actions did indeed speak louder than words. And he would have followed through, forgetting for a time, the times with Evelyn—had it not been for Jenny's call. And now a time of reckoning was at hand, as if destined, part of the developing scripts of all their lives.

§

He and Evelyn took their seats on the bride's side, about half way down from the altar. He could see Odelia and, he guessed, her husband, weighed down by a professional looking camera bag, just a few rows ahead on the same side of the church. Rory sucked at his pricked finger, almost nibbling it, nervously drawing on it, and he thought first of Odelia's kisses, and then Evelyn's—and, remembering his own marriage, fantasized what the groom would remember of Jenny's kiss, wondering if it would be an innocent, friendly kiss or a hot passionate one and whether, embarrassed, she would push him away.

The ceremony was what could be expected in outline: large Catholic church on the West side, Jenny's cousins at the registry by the door, altar candles, pretty bridesmaids—especially Evelyn, although her corsage had an akimbo droop to it, which he sorely regretted—crew cut best man, a darling ring bearer, muscular, solicitous ushers, a tall priest with a Castilian accent, and two sets of love-lit eyes darting back and forth, through tears and handkerchiefs.

Mostly Rory paid attention to the approaching rainstorm and the thunder rolling in over the volcanoes from the north west, and the back of Odelia's head, her still blonde but not quite so vibrant hair, and her feathery hat—he didn't know quite what to call it but it gave her a classy air, a look of money and a life of comfortable means, allowing her to wear what he could tell was an up to the minute stylish chapeau, reminding him of past times in church with his mother and her collection of pretty hats.

She wore a rose-colored jacket that fit her snugly with two long, tapering darts coming back over her shoulder blades. He remembered lifting her coat collar from the back, taking it off slowly, and tossing it on the divan, staring at her neck and blouse, and all the while her chest. Then he remembered again, such a monumental act, unbuttoning her blouse that first night and pulling down the straps of her slip and letting her full, soft, white breasts rest naturally on her chest, rising and falling with each gasping breath.

"Are you sure? He remembered asking. "Do you want to?" And her saying breathlessly, "I do! Yes, I do"!

And then the priest's words, "I pronounce you man and wife. You may kiss the bride, "brought him back to the present. Then the organ. And then the exodus. Odelia said something to her husband, and then walked away while he readied his camera. Rory could barely look up to see Odelia's face as she passed him alone, her veil covering her beautiful, pained face, her muted yet glimmering lips, and her hand reaching up with a tissue to wipe away the tears—of what nature he could not tell.

"It could have been us," he thought, and wondered if she thought any thing like that and whether or not she had noticed him in any way similar to the way he noticed her, thinking about her with such conflicted longing, regret and resignation.

The bride and groom dashed out of the church under a large blue and gray golfing umbrella provided by the attentive, ever ready ushers. The rain was hard and although the hotel where the reception was to be held was only a few miles away, over the West Central bridge and up Rio Grande Boulevard, the rain made for slow going—impossible to caravan with cars leaving at different times, taking alternate routes, and drivers and passengers generally laughing and talking, ready to kick up their heels like horses in a storm, thinking of possible testimonials and toasts, rather than concentrating on best routes.

On their mad escape, Rory and Evelyn had little to say about the ceremony other than Evelyn's characteristic complaints—getting her feet wet and ruining her shoes, and a tirade on Rory's overall clumsiness.

This damn corsage! It's bothered me since the start. If I didn't still have to take photos with the wedding party I'd throw it into the river. What's more, you drive just about like you pin on flowers. Can you even see where you're going with these worn out windshield wipers? We need to trade in this goddamn antique jalopy! We'll probably stall somewhere along the road for Christ's sake."

"Like that Jaguar, there on the shoulder," Rory said! "Isn't that Richard and Vanessa Brown? The Pizza King himself and his 'all the toppings' wife? No jalopy there you know, just British luxury engineering... or the results of chunks of Limburger cheese on the block. I can smell it now. Whoa ho! Make that an extra large with extra cheese, Dick!"

"You and your juvenile grease-monkey friends! Did you and Bonnell gunk up the engine on that beautiful car? You and your river rat friends are too much to deal with, that's for certain! Always lost back in high school!"

Even so, the jalopy and the bickering couple made it to the hotel portico before most of the other revelers and Rory let his chattering wife out hearing first the car door slam shut on her umbrella, then her grumbling against the thunder, "Damn rain. Damn cheap car. Stupid toy umbrella! I'll try to catch up with you after all the photos are taken. Now I have to tidy up again. Try not to drink too many bottles of beer!"

"Beer!" Rory hooted. "Who said anything about beer? This is a night for brandy, a host bar and an old girl friend somewhere on the premises ready to kiss me or kick my ass," and he swung the souped up old '58 Impala he'd pampered for years into the first parking space he found and made his worrisome way in a beeline for the bar. And he thought again of Delia and that slow, snowy drive along the very same boulevard, those several years past and wondered what he would say when they finally talked.

§

The scurry of moving the reception inside due to the rain was still underway when Rory entered the lobby, and, following the information given at the desk, he walked over to the dining hall. Few people were there yet, other than the serving staff scuttling back and forth.

There she was...at a big table off to the side by herself. She looked up and saw him, expecting someone else, maybe her husband. Her sip of wine turned into a gulp when he waved and smiled.

"That's not a diet coke from Lionel's, is it? Not even a favorite Patrón margarita from El Pinto? "

"No, Chardonnay these days," she said. "But you remember the El Pinto margaritas?"

"I remember just about everything between us, be it booze or bliss. Or kiss. I still drive my old Chevy in remembrance of you. It's been a long ride, a long old time leading to this?"

"Yes, a long, lost time."

"Want me to bring you another glass of wine? I need a drink myself."

"No, sit and talk. Let me flag down the waiter who brought me my wine. He's young and good-looking. Reminds me not so much of someone but that lost time we were talking about. Here he comes, what do you want?"

"Make it the house brandy a double...but tell me all about you, Delia. Where's your husband? I assume that was your husband I saw you with."

"He's with your wife, I assume, taking her picture. He's the photographer for the reception, the drive away, everything but the honeymoon. He did the church photos before the ceremony."

"Kind of ironic. Me here with you. Him there with her. So tell me...."

"You tell me. Last thing I remember was finding a dozen yellow roses on my porch, reading the 'Dear Delia' note, bursting into tears, and locking myself in my bedroom much to the dismay of my brother who didn't know what to think."

"Yes. I've carried the memory of those roses around with me most days and just about every night, especially around three or four o'clock in the morning, when the thorns make themselves felt again and the bloom fades in slow motion from the petals."

"Good. At least I wanted you to feel some of my pain for the first months, even the first couple of years. Then I married Vince and forgot for a while, until I had a real affair of the heart and that pain of heart failure, real as the thunder storm outside, was rougher."

"Affair of the heart? You mean heart attack! When was that?"

"Just last year. See...double coronary bypass. Doctor Matthews at Lovelace. Best in the West. At least he saved me."

Rory took a long sniff of his brandy, held his breath and grimaced as she unbuttoned the top buttons on her blouse and exposed the scar, long and pinkish-purple and reminding him of the centipedes he found around his childhood home.

"God sakes, Delia! You're lucky, I guess. I mean, that they fixed things. Repercussions all around I would guess."

"Diet, exercise, pills, and regular checkups. Some lingering heartache, if you know what I mean," And she slowly began buttoning her blouse. He wanted to stop her and place his hand on her chest, caress the scar into disappearing.

She was so thin, so gaunt, nothing like he remembered and he couldn't help thinking how he felt when he first saw and felt her breasts, his hand there where the scar was now, and he could hear the palpitations of his own heart in his ears, and he reflexively put down his brandy and placed one hand over his own heart, and asked, "May I? I must!" And without any consent other than the yes in her eyes put his other hand gently on her chest.

"Life has its ways, doesn't it? Its lessons? But don't think for a minute that I would go back, back before the roses. Vince kept me well supplied with roses while I was recuperating. Red roses, dark, red roses. Blood roses. The American Beauty kind. And you? Tell me about you and where your choice, I should say where your choices have taken you," and she reached over and placed her hand on his, the hard metal of their wedding rings touching then glancing off each other.

He reached for the brandy, took another long whiff, then a couple of big sips and said, "Still chasing the dream, I guess, although I'm not sure what the original dream was or still is. I work as a bookkeeper part time, take some classes at the university—trying to get certified to teach—and I play most weekends in a band, you know, bars, restaurants, private parties I just show up wherever the piano player says."

"You still play the guitar? Still sing? Remember those songs you used to sing to me out on the mesa—me, you, your guitar? I still remember those nights, and that Eddy Arnold, Jim Reeves mesa music, with fondness."

" I do. Old standards mostly and some country songs I first listened to on the café jukebox and the radio when a kid. Took lessons from a nightclub musician. And his stripper girl friend. Dear old Jerry and Margaret!"

"Wish I could hear you sing some of those songs again in the way you used to sing them—before the roses came."

"One rose, one song for every time I broke your heart? Little did I know I was sending them to myself." And he recited the lyrics he used to sing, "I'll hold you in my heart, till I can hold you in my arms. So, darlin' please wait for me."

"How sweet," she said. "Thank you. It took me some time but now I'm glad we were able to break each other's heart. At least we have the memories, the good tempered with the bad, but ever lasting."

"Better to have loved and lost sort of thing? I'm not so sure about that. But look, people are starting to come back and all the revelry will kick up any minute. My wife will walk through that door, and so will your husband and...."

"He'll be busy taking pictures for the duration. A wedding like this means big money for him, for us, so maybe I can get him to take a 'blind' picture, so to speak, of you and me, for old time sake, for the ages. I've never told him about you, just another boyfriend as far as he's concerned. You talk about me all the time to your wife I'll bet."

"Nope. Kind of a secret love in that respect. So any photos would be laced not only with chardonnay and brandy but with tough irony."

"Speak of the devils, here they come, your wife, my husband, all the bridesmaids, the best man, the groom, the parents, and cousins and sisters—the entire parade, including shades of ourselves. Lives begun and ended. Helloes and goodbyes. And here we are 'two lonely people' now in a crowd. And 'so much in love we have to say goodnight,' but never goodbye, just adieu, not as long as there are roses to smell, to press, and to remember."

"A rose isn't just a rose, is it?" Rory said, and leaned over to kiss her.

"And a kiss isn't just a kiss," she replied, remembering his lips as they met hers.

Readers Guide

"Twilight Troubadour"

1. Do you see the relationship between Rory and Jerry as good?

2. Is Jerry's nightclub lifestyle a bad influence on the boy?

3. Can a musical instrument such as Jerry's or Rory's guitar have a personality separate and apart from a musician playing it? Or does it take on the voice and emotions of the musician?

4. Why is the guitar associated so much with the West and its cowboy traditions?

5. Is Rory's damage to his guitar related to the jukebox damage? Compare or contrast.

6. How does meeting a musician like Mel Tormé, so different in style than Jerry, affect Rory?

7. Are Jerry and Roy plausible friends? Anything archetypal about their relationship?

8. Do you see Smitty and Mrs. Curly as villains resisting Rory's and Jerry's heroism?

9. Can Rory's seeming crush on Margaret suggest a kind of platonic ménage a trois with Jerry?

10. Most maturation stories intimate a certain happy/sad, hello/goodbye ambivalence. Is that at play here?

11. Is it believable for Margaret to represent all women to Rory?

"Uncle Nabob, Milo, and Me"

1. Sidekicks usually get along. What leads to strained relations between the narrator and Milo?

2. Which counts the most in the South Valley locale of the story—heredity or environment?

3. Contrast Milo's discourse on Tex Ritter with Mrs. Gonzales's lesson on Tchaikovsky. What's at work here?

4. How does Rory resist his mother's snobbery? Is she truly a snob?

5. Does Rory mind Milo's poverty-stricken house and relatives? Do the boys realize their class differences?

6. Does Milo's air rifle bring the two boys closer together or does animosity develop because of it?

7. Comment on the boys' differing values about birds.

8. Should some kind of social service be called about Uncle Nabob and Laney?

9. Are Milo and Rory at different levels of puberty? How so?

10. How does the picnic fun play against the nearby, restricted nuclear weapons stronghold?

11. Does the name of Uncle Nabob and his lingering memory suggest pleasure or pain to Rory?

"Lucinda and the Wild Birds"

1. Does the fact that Rory has favorite birds and is protective of them endear him to the reader or does it matter in building the plot?

2. What traits, positive or negative, are associated with goats, Chano, and his patriarchy?

3. What is suggested by introducing Lucinda as having cruel but loving ways? A soft and a hard-sounding name? How does this duality work out in the resolution of the story?

4. Does the retrospective point of view indicate certain lessons learned? What kind of lessons?

5. There is an Edenic quality suggested in the meeting of Rory and Lucinda. Why is such a setting effective?

6. How is Lavola a foil to Lucinda in her way of ringing chickens' necks?

7. How credible is the reaction of Lucinda and Rory to Milo's shooting the flicker?

8. Why does Lucinda kill the nest full of birds and justify it in such an ironic, shocking way?

"House Call"

1. Is Rory's physical injury tragic or comic to him? To the reader?

2. Is Satherine credible as a folk doctor or curandera capable of talking with animals?

3. What is the Duende and what role does it play?

4. Do you like Mr. Mitchell because of or in spite of his portrayal?

5. Are the setting and the Strayhope lifestyle appealing? Why?

6. Is the boy's paralysis real or psychosomatic because of the polio scare?

7. Is Rory's nightmare worse than his injury or somehow part of it?

8. Would you be willing to analyze the dream, and is its thematic interpretation/interpolation structurally useful?

9. Is the story a testament to the power of prayer and mysticism or merely entertainment?

10. Some readers might see this as a Christmas story. Would that be a misreading?

"The Good Samaritan"

1. Is there anything to the ironic stereotype of a deacon's kid going wrong?

2. A church deacon with a mechanical voice box sounds rather demonic. Is it an over the top characterization?

3. Some might think this story too harsh on evangelical clergy and congregations. Is the satire offensive to you?

4. Is little Dirk incorrigible? Just born bad, headed down the road to perdition and beyond salvation?

5. Who was Roberta Sherwood?

6. Wherein lies the irony in contrasting Sunshine Mountain to Battleship Rock?

7. Is Little Dirk a convincing Christian bully?

8. Do all the boys share in the death of Wilson Hoffiens? Or just the narrator?

9. Do you see the story as a cynical inversion of the story of the Good Samaritan?

10. Is this story an endorsement of capital punishment?

"Smitten"

1. What era do the aircraft and drive-in theater represent?

2. In what sense is this or is this not a Romeo and Juliet love story?

3. Does Rory's like of fast cars and fast planes and violating a fire code make him a juvenile delinquent?

4. Is fixing a traffic ticket really such a bad thing? Is it indicative of Rory's flaws or municipal corruption?

5. Should Rory have declined Thanksgiving dinner at the D.A.'s house?

6. Guns play a role here both in hunting and protection. Is it a pro-gun story or a cautionary tale about them?

7. Do you at all sympathize with Mr. Metcalf's treatment of his son and alcoholic wife?

8. Is Rory's calling Mr. Metcalf a "dumb ass" a severe enough pronouncement?

9. What connects the fire hose scene with the undercooked turkey dinner scene?

10. Explain the thematic appropriateness of the title.

"Pachuco"

1. Is public middle school as profane, crude, and violent as portrayed?

2. Here Anglos (stompers and squadros or nerds) square off against pachucos in gang-like groups. Is the current school scene really just as dangerous and just as disruptive?

3. Is a preemptive blow to the face a good strategy and advice or just dirty fighting?

4. Should Eddie Quintana be seen as a hero or a traitor?

5. How and why does Martha Goss bring all groups together?

6. Is the cruelty toward disadvantaged kids like Larry and Martha universal?

7. The narrator's conscience gets him in trouble. Is his stand stupid or heroic?

8. Is corporal punishment for fighting justified? Effective? Cruel?

9. Are Eddie and his entourage more comedic than heroic?

10. Is Eddie more assimilated into the Anglo culture or Rory into the Hispanic culture?

"Trophy Girl"

1. Did you ever know a person like Leo Gibbs?

2. Is Leo more of a stalker or a so-called "wolf?" Can you justify his seductions?

3. Should or shouldn't this "battle of the sexes" relationship favor Celia Vargas rather than Leo?

4. Is Celia to blame for falling for Leo's enticements? No "blame" either way?

5. Is being a trophy girl more expansively metaphorical than portrayed here?

6. What does this story say about sexuality and advertising?

7. Do too many young women fall victim to such chauvinistic romancing?

8. Are the implicit values of the story still deemed misguided?

9. Are the new and old cars emblematic of changing moral times?

"Yearbook"

1. Is the narrator's tone angry, mean spirited, or just disappointed?

2. Is Rory's rationale for going on a double date with Darlene and Larry merely a matter of heart over head?

3. Why don't names seem to matter or not matter to Darlene?

4. Are the allusions to all the stars of horror movies a lost reference today?

5. Why is the story seemingly so obsessed with names?

6. How does advertising help date this "double date?"

7. Is Joan's description of her abortion appropriate on her date with Rory?

8. Is Rory's response to such a description just too disrespectful?

9. Is jumping off the hay wagon a cowardly thing to do? Why does Rory enlist Larry to jump with him?

10. Is Rory's yearbook "To Irene" inscription a work of genius? Characterize it.

"Hell Canyon"

1. How is the epigraph related to the story?

2. What's the rhetorical effect of the long first sentence in the second paragraph?

3. How does the exoticism (i.e., stranger in a strange land) of the opening scene strike you?

4. Does meeting Lavola more fully here lead you to like or dislike her?

5. Why does she offer Rita a job so quickly?

6. What happened to the missing bodies in the train wreck?

7. Anything unusual about the turquoise ring gift and its giver?

8. What's the appeal of going to such an ominous sounding hunting ground as Hell Canyon?

9. What do you take from the rituals of the funeral and the hunt? Authentically primitive or New Age replication?

10. Why does Rory have to endure his injury and ghostly encounters alone.

"Chigger"

1. What's the difference between pretending to be a hunter and actually being one?

2. Is the imagistic correspondence between a chigger and a drop of blood convincing?

3. How is Rory's dream contextualized by hunting?

4. Is the calf killing by Juan a foreshadowing? How so?

5. What's at the root of the tension between Lavola and Billy Sue?

6. Is the avuncular relationship between Rory and Willard archetypal?

7. What goes on between Virgil and Billy Sue? Where is Lavola in this?

8. How does the quail in the brush pile metaphorically explain Rory's lonely wish?

9. Whose shot kills the first buck?

10. What does the rivalry between Willard and B.J. echo?

11. Why is finding the second dead deer a turning point for Rory?

12. Does flirtatious Billy Sue reap her just reward?

"Yellow Roses"

1. "What if?" is a theme in this story. Had it been different would it have been better? What's the use of memories?

2. Is jilting essentially a cowardly act or can it ever be mitigated?

3. What are the connotations of gardenias and of yellow roses?

4. Does Rory really regret his decision or accept it?

5. Is Rory made out to be a Walter Mitty victim to a shrewish wife?

6. Where's the irony of the three couples meeting at the wedding?

7. How do Vince's red roses contrast with Rory's?

8. What justifies Rory placing his hand on Delia's chest? Kissing her?

9. How does this story compare with other forsaken love stories you've read?

CPSIA information can be obtained
at www.ICGtesting.com
Printed in the USA
FSHW010155071219
64669FS